Escape

from
Within

Escape from Within

from

a fictional story by
Maryse Augustin

XULON PRESS

Xulon Press
2301 Lucien Way #415
Maitland, FL 32751
407.339.4217
www.xulonpress.com

Unless otherwise indicated, Scripture quotations taken from the Holy Bible, New Living Translation (NLT). Copyright ©1996, 2004, 2007 by Tyndale House Foundation. Used by permission of Tyndale House Publishers, Inc.

Paperback ISBN-13: 978-1-6628-2041-0

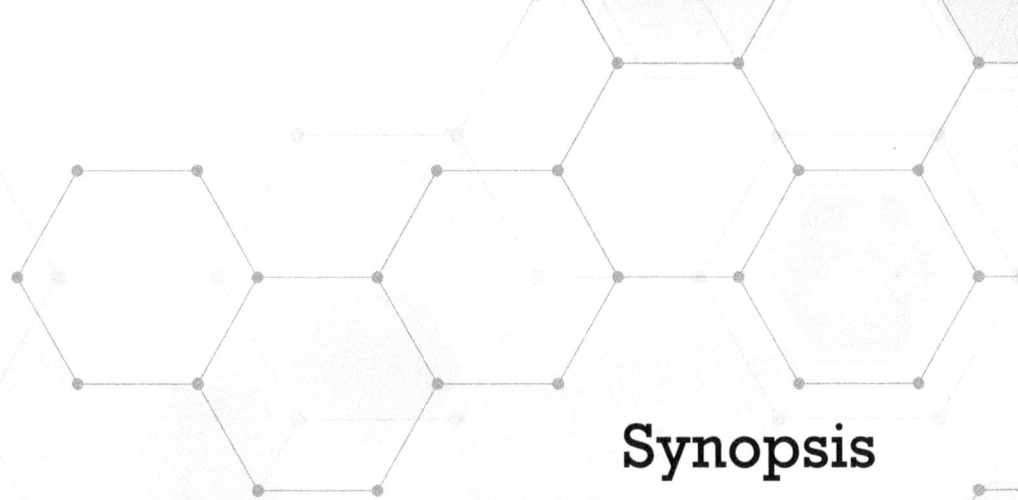

Synopsis

A mother with a somewhat successful marriage has 3 daughters. On a daily basis, she reexamines her life and analyzes every word uttered by her husband of 18 years. She devises a plan to escape. As this quest for relief takes the form of departure from her home, with her 3 daughters, because of her husband's possible deceit, daily verbiage, and bothersome ways, will she return, or will she be able to escape? Several twists and turns will be experienced. The story explores her rationale, and the motivation behind her decision to leave her home.

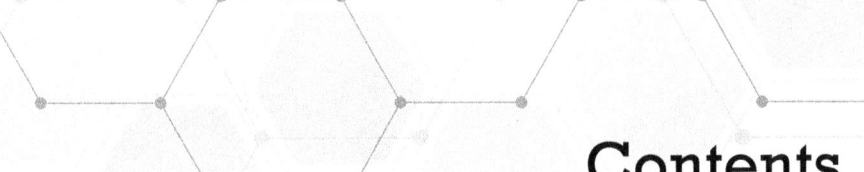

Contents

Introduction

Ideally, most women who marry, do so, for stability, culture, values, and normal standards of living. Fortunately for some, their unions result in a successful binding of the two, and the family that they create. Whether it be due to a boring routine or a lifeless courtship, some so-called successful marriages do not exemplify the norm that certain women crave for.

In my personal life, my mom at times would explain the comfort that comes from a unified family and the respect therefrom, because mostly of expectations, acceptance of society and the guaranty that loneliness would potentially be nonexistent through such a creation and upholding of the vows. I remember hearing at times, that a marriage is comparable to winning the lottery. A good marriage representative of an ideal way of thinking, manners of respecting, and communicating, trusting, and all other perks signifying strengths of normalcy, is indeed a state of being to cherish and retain.

The story, Escape from within, takes into account the facts surrounding a woman's state of mind. It explores the ramifications of acting, and not acting on one's insights. It also exemplifies what becomes of the most miniscule and petty observations of a mate, relative to his/her partner in life.

Although my personal experience as it relates to retaining a marriage, has been detrimental, (being a divorced woman), my treatment of this story is based on objectivity, with no personal bias. As I face challenges as a fictional writer, and though I have yet to establish a strong readership, I take comfort in acknowledging that hope, above all else matters. Most importantly, I write to reinforce my faith, and for therapeutic purposes. My hope is to engage readers after the entire book has been published. Feedback is encouraged. A review, no matter how derived, would be appreciated. Many thanks to my readers, and to the Lord.

This story is completely fictional. Any similarities in names, and circumstances in the story line, are purely coincidental.

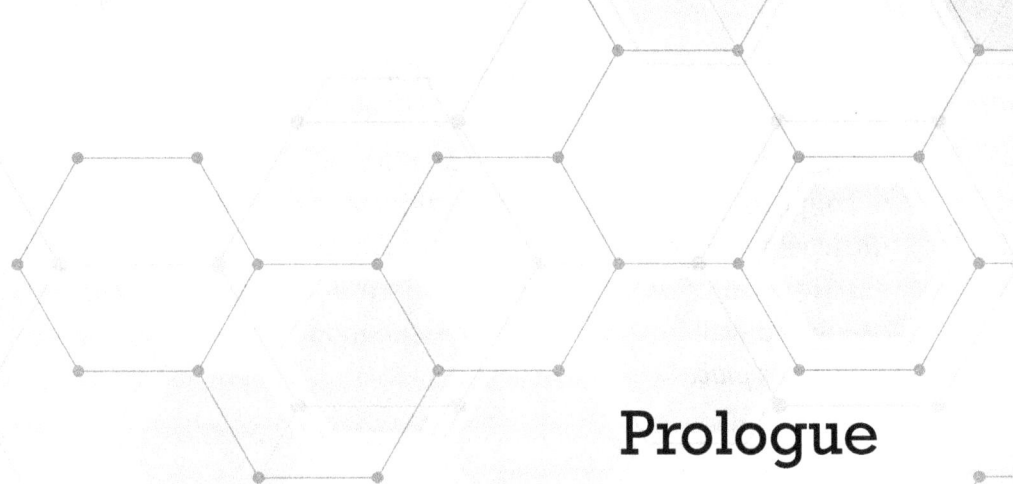

Prologue

Streaming along the water banks of her area, she was deep in thoughts about everything that concerned herself and her family. Having had a good life, from valuing her career, nurturing her children toward achieving excellence academically, to wanting more and more from her husband, her mental captivity tormented her at times to the point of slight insanity.

Her slow pace in her walk routines allowed her mind to wander about incidents of her current days, as well as those of yesteryears. The instance she began to distrust her husband was primarily on her mind. *"Why would he withhold such information?so silly...a bonus of $35,000...big deal...Why was that so irrelevant in our daily conversations. Perhaps he needed to hide this for a specific reason. But, What?"* Her thoughts trailed into other things. *"I thought we resumed a normal life since that "cheap"incident. He simply does not get it"*

So, her thoughts made sense only to herself as she strolled along her route, from her neigborhood meeting, to her house. Then, something startled her. A beam of lights was blinding as it approached closer. She walked closely to the curb, wanting to avoid getting slammed by this slow approaching car; then she began to realize that it was her husband's automobile. He stopped as he rolled down his passenger side window, to chat with his wife. "I'll be back in a little while. I have to run a couple of errands" She waved with a smile."I'll see you in a little while, then."

He sped off within the speed limit allowed. As she continued to walk toward her house, she mumbled..."*I will soon leave this place.*"

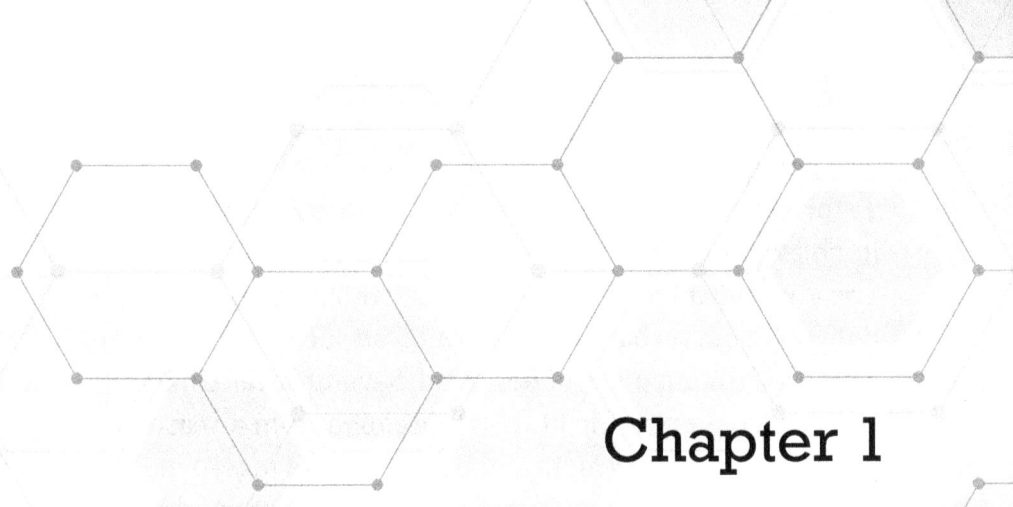

Chapter 1

Thoughts trailing
Thoughts expressed
Path of peace reeling
Forceful needs addressed

Mota, was a well exposed woman of grace, who had been married to her husband for 18 years. Having had the best that life could offer through her upbringing, she remained humble throughout her life. As a middle Aged woman, her mantra was basically aimed at continuing to excel in her field. A multi talented self employed Executive, who specializes in conducting all types of training for other executives, ranging from diversity training, to social etiquette protocols, based on studies analyzed globally. Her three daughters, Tori, Biamu (who are 18 year old twins) and Sino, 17, inherited her powerful spirits of academia, as well as tenacity and assertiveness.

All three, for the most part, sided with their mother on any types of debates concerning family inputs. One particular negativity arose at one time and resulted in all three leaving the house, trailing behind their mother, who decided to walk rather than taking her car to get away from Roi. From the disagreement, according to the three, Roi was out of order. He was being disrespectful when he referred to Mota's sister as a storyteller, rather than an author. "She is no author...Never in her wildest dreams will she receive respect from the literary world...blah blah blah..."Tori, who assumed the older twin position, verbalized her opinion on such an outburst and gave her father a piece of her mind. Several other similar outbursts were very difficult to comprehend from a reasonable point of view, driving Mota at times into a fit of rage, pondering how and when she would escort her daughters and herself away from Roi.

In most cultures, good marriages entail a somewhat incomplete understanding of the other partner. For instance, it takes a great deal of courage for a man to admit in full force what he thinks of his sister in law. No matter how difficult it can be to absorb the insult, the thoughts are actually expressed to stand on a certain platform. The question is – what led to such a line and trend of thinking?

In their upbringing, Mota's three children shared a common belief, as a result of their mother's attention to failure more so than any other types of sentiments. She ceaselessly taught them to understand the value of differences in people's way of life as well as any intrinsic and unseen/undetected virtues. In any story, there lay a hidden meaning, from her point of view. From this concept, whatever was on the surface was simply not the whole picture. She always instilled the importance of discussions, no matter how small and insignificant.

Tori, particularly inherited most of these traits. In her development, her pet peeves were pronounced tremendously, especially when she engaged in reading certain novels that brought out emotional issues. One of which dealt with a Cinderella (so to speak) story that turned out to be less than formidable for the subject. It involved the maltreatment of a servant whose path certainly dictated possibilities of greatness. The village in which she resided misdiagnosed her problem, then sentenced her to life of servitude to her stepsisters. Not only did she not gain the affection of a so called prince, she became enslaved for a long time under the direction of the two wicked ladies. Tori simply could not understand how, after so many complaints to her local officials in her village, that she had to endure such atrocities. These atrocities included a secretive network that aimed to block every action that she undertook for any possible endeavor. Tori was expressive in maintaining her stance on fairness; but she also enjoyed a good ending relative to fiction as well as nonfiction.

Biamu was mostly interested in law, and attended certain types of court proceedings just to acclimate herself in that type of environment. She was very attentive to summary judgments of any kind. One that particularly resonated with her was a summary that dealt with extreme cruelty. "*..To my surprise, you don't seem to have any regrets for everything that's happened here. Is there a possibility of redemption of any kind from you, as a member of society? What will you ask for when you request mercy five to seven years from now? Will you understand the parole board's position on your request? Have you anything to say? Never mind..., you've said it all with the grin on your face. You thoroughly enjoyed your numerous actions against this person, haven't you? Even if I were to sentence you for life, it would not be enough punishment for you to understand the gravity of your actions. First and foremost, I want to thank the jury for its verdict..*"

Biamu sat there, taking notes on her pad, and even recorded the facial expressions of the defendant as the judge continued his judgment. But, one thing in particular bothered her to the point of fright. "*What if this defendant is just one of a string of the same because he does seem to feel that he'll be out in society in just a few months, judging from his demeanor."* Biamu's trend of thoughts stemmed primarily from innocence and lack of a broader platform of exposure. At her age, she knew that one day she would become an attorney, defending all sorts of criminals. From sitting in courtrooms, and jotting down her own perspectives on things gave her a front row view of what her career would be like.

Sino, was the most spiritual of the three. Everything that concerned life in general, from her viewpoints, had a direct correlation to the bible. She was particularly judgmental somewhat, when her father greatly criticized one of her mom's relatives for taking in a stranger as an adoptee. She fully understood the rationale for such action on the part of her aunt, who incidentally was robbed by the same person. It began when Aunt Tam was feeling down one night, not having had a good day. Her son came home with an attitude, and was slightly disrespectful to her slamming the door while she was trying to express a thought to him. Slightly depressed, she went to the living room and sat on the couch. A few minutes of deep thinking passed when she heard some noise in her basement. The manner in which her mother explained this story to her was explicit in that she felt moved so much by the story that she expressed discontent with her father when he denounced the actions of Aunt Tam. When she heard the noise in the basement, she assumed it was her husband; then went toward where the noise originated. As she approached, calling out her husband's name..."Ralph, is that you, down there? Ralph? She didn't hear any answers. She flipped the light switch, and saw a young man, with a gun in his hand. "Lady, I need money, tell me where the money is." Startled by what she was seeing, a young guy, with a leather jacket, a small black hoodie over his head, with clenched jaws. She responded, "How much were you looking for?you can't go around trespassing on people's property, asking for money, you should have rung the bell, and asked, I would have done everything I could to help you out ."He seemed impatient and said: "Look, lady, I don't want to hurt you, but you need to listen and give me about $500, otherwise I don't know what I'll do..."After saying how much he needed, Aunt Tam turned around and said, "Ok, follow me..., I'll give you more than $500...why would a young handsome boy like you be robbing folks for a few bucks like that...don't you have a family?"As she walked up the stairs, while asking questions, she was not worried about the gun going off, she simply made up her mind that what he was asking for was not that much. He followed her closely, and became somewhat worried it was some sort of trick. He mumbled a few words as he walked close to her from behind. She opened her bedroom door, slid her hand in her top drawer and took out cash from an envelope. As she began to count the cash, he snatched it from her hand. He looked around to see if he would or could snatch anything else. She sadly said, "I have a safe that I can open. I keep much more in there. She didn't even wait for him to agree, she walked over to the safe, opened it and offered him the path to go and snatch whatever he wanted. Psychologically, a robber with that type of ease of robbing someone tends to be mistrusting. He had a small duffel bag.took it out from under his jacket, placed the money in the envelope in the bag, then cleaned out the safe. Oh his way out, he looked back at the lady, sitting on the edge of her bed, somewhat disturbed emotionally, said "thank you", and ran out with his loot.

At that point of the story, Sino had quite a few questions for her mother, such as why did she offer much more than he was asking for? How come she wasn't frightened? But, she kept remembering the rest of the story.

A few weeks passed. Aunt Tam was alone at home when she heard her doorbell. She opened her door and saw a handsome black fellow, dressed in casual clothes that looked expensive. His appearance was impressive. As soon as she saw him, she knew it was him. She didn't feel afraid, and said "Yes, may I help you?"He responded with a mumble that Tam didn't understand. "I am sorry, son, let me ask you again, what can I do for you? With tears streaming down his cheeks, he responded by saying, "I am sorry...here..."He handed her a paper bag filled with her jewelry, money, and bonds which were all part of the loot he had stolen from her. She took it, looked at the contents and became emotional. She kept her door open, and walked in to sit by a small table in the foyer. "You must have a story. I am all ears" He was sobbing, explaining that he had to do what he did. "I had to get away from my stepfather. He kept beating on my mom and my little sister"

"But, that's not the way to resolve a problem like that"

"You don't understand. If I had rung the bell and asked, you would not have taken me seriously"

"I probably would have offered some way to help you. So you're looking good, what now?"

"I just wanted to say I was sorry for the way I entered your home. I've never met anyone like you. You're a very nice lady. I hope you can forgive me"

"Forgiven! I must confess to you, that the day you came here, was one of the best days of my life. I can't fully explain what I mean. But, thank you for returning these things."

"Ok. Bye"

"Good Bye"

Chapter 1

She closed the door after him; and simply could not believe he had returned most of the things taken.

On the day of the robbery, her son's demeanor changed for the better. Earlier on in the day, his disrespectful ways almost terrified her to the point of depression. As soon as he heard that his mom had been robbed, he became protective to the point of ridiculousness. He took a baseball bat and headed on the streets, looking for the robber; then returned and made tea for her mom. From Tam's viewpoints, such an incident was designed so that her son would change his ways. Several months after the robbery, Tam asked around everywhere, to be made apprised of her robber's family, friends and all that concerned him. After asking around, and reporting to child and family services, she finally found out all that she needed to know about this young man. He was then living in foster homes, being switched left and right. After placing a petition to adopt him, she finally got her wish and he became her son.

As Sino remembered this tale, she became more and more convinced that somehow, the incident was a design from a higher power. Not only did this young man excel in school, he devised an approach to help his sister in her daily living, through constant contacts, and family bonding.

Roi never understood the rationale behind such action. He surmised on most occasions, that it was a plot to rob Tam, and keep her under his control. Sino, seriously disagreed, and even at times suggested that the whole family not absorb her father's stance on things.

Along with other family tales, upon which one side of certain viewpoints would be Roi's, alone; and the other side, all 4, (Mota and her 3 daughters), the Tam tale was pronounced on their minds, with extreme disagreement against Roi's position.

On the day, Mota's thoughts dictated the possibility of simply leaving and never returning, Tori suggested a "lockdown", against her father.

"What do you mean?"

"First of all, he is creeping me out, every time he extremely disagrees with anything we have to say. A lockdown from him will work. We will stay on one side of the house, while he stays on the other side."

"That won't work. You know how he comes into contact with us, with a grin on his face, wanting to challenge every word"

"But, seriously, Mom, Dad has to change. When he says he has a "couple of errands"to run, it usually means a night of fun with his friends, no matter what kind of plans we have…"

"I know. What you are saying is so minor. You don't know what I am going through in this relationship"

The thoughts that were traveling in Mota's head placed her somewhere, four years prior.

They were away on vacation, in the Caribbean. After spending two glorious days, enjoying each other, on the third day, mayhem ensued. They were sitting on the beach, when a tall, dark and handsome man approached Mota, to compliment her on her looks. Although it seemed innocent enough that he would do so in front of her husband, her reaction appeared flirtatious to Roi. In response to his compliments, Roi blurted out "Why don't you two get a room, huh." Mota felt embarrassed as he kept screaming out the same line. As the gentleman walked away, she became so furious, that she wanted to leave right then and stopped her vacation. "How obnoxious"! she mumbled under her breath, and walked away to reach her room. That day was an unforgivable day, as she kept revisiting the reasons why she married him in the first place. *"He wasn't that way when I met him, was he? How could he be so freaking annoying...he embarrassed me..."* Such an incident became one of many incidents that kept building up over the years.

As Mota was remembering that incident, Sino was on the phone with a member of her bible study class. Mota slowly drifted back to the present, hearing Sino's side of the conversation. Overhearing the conversation was effortless; since she was not too far from where her mom was chatting with Tori... The exchange sounded personal from the point of advising her listener..."since you don't feel comfortable with your predicament, I don't think you should settle into it. Anything that doesn't feel right, usually, isn't...oh wait a minute."the conversation stopped as Sino placed her right hand over the receiver..."Mom, Dad is listening to my conversation. I can hear the click, and his breathing...he keeps saying yes, I agree, blah blah blah.., mom, can you please put a stop to this. He cannot continue invading my space, like this...Dad, get off the phone, please,"as she removed her hand, and advised her fellow bible class member, she would call her back.

Mota approached her daughter, to ask if she was all right. Pacing back and forth, she kept her feelings to herself, but asking how he returned from his errands without her being alerted. She looked outside the kitchen window, and noticed his car in the driveway. *"It could be a middle age crisis..., I can't bear this anymore...,* she was thinking out loud, as Sino crossed her arms to ask, "what now?"

She motioned Sino to stop so she could think. Her thoughts trailed between staying with lockdown standards, or leave and rent a seasonal place for herself and her three girls.

From life's developments, certain people have the luxury to exercise a choice when there's such a possibility. In Mota's case, she clearly had the financial resources, after 18 years of marriage, to commence a lifestyle, away from her husband. As she kept contemplating her choices, her trends of thoughts were interrupted by a phone call from a close friend. Sino handed the phone to her…"Mom, it's Sti, on the phone for you."She handed the phone and walked away. "Hello Sti, so good to hear from you"

"You left the meeting earlier today, without saying Bye, so I am just reaching out to you, just in case you need me"

"Oh, no, I am fine…, so how did the meeting end?"

"Great! We have our new watchdogs, to upgrade security of our neighborhood, and we're thinking about nominating you for community president…, you really need to just think about it…we're not looking for an answer right away."

"Well, I'll tell you what, now is not a good time to be nominated for anything"

"Why not? What's wrong?"

"let's put it this way, I no longer feel that I have the strength to plan anymore…, but, surely, there's really no urgency…, just keep the nomination open for now…, and I am really appreciative of your thoughtful suggestion"

"I understand. I want you to know that I am here, if you need to talk about anything"

"I'll keep it in mind. Thank you for calling, and I'll keep in touch"

"Ok, then, So long"

Sti was one of Mota's best friends. She didn't feel she had the courage to continue to complain to her about her husband's annoying demeanor. She knew she would hear…*"does he give you reason to believe that he has a mistress? Does he abuse you or your kids? Does he keep garbage all over the house? Does he gamble large sums of money to distress you over possible loss of assets? Does he abuse his body in any way?"*She knew she would have to keep answering "no"to all of the above. What Sti didn't know was that other things that mattered in life could be just as enticing to overcome as the points she would actually bring to the surface. Mota never told her about important incidents such as a committee meeting Roi had to attend, in his job capacity, in which his decision was crucial. The essence of his analysis in that decision lay the foundation for some-one's life and future. It was a plagiarism case which had to be decided. She also never told her about his patronizing a cheating husband, and actually rationalized to justify his base-less actions; she also never told her about his horrifying position on the landmark case, Roe v Wade; and never told her his stance on – No education for immigrants–. Her thinking placed her at every instance at that particular juncture of the discussion on each topic. She wondered at times, if her husband had somehow mentally transformed over the years.

As a working woman, whose life and mind were shaped through the escalating evolution for women's rights, her stance was always felt to be one of feminism. As sad as it may have been to her, her husband's true personality became more pronounced over time. She knew something had to be done, not only for herself and her children, but also for Roi.

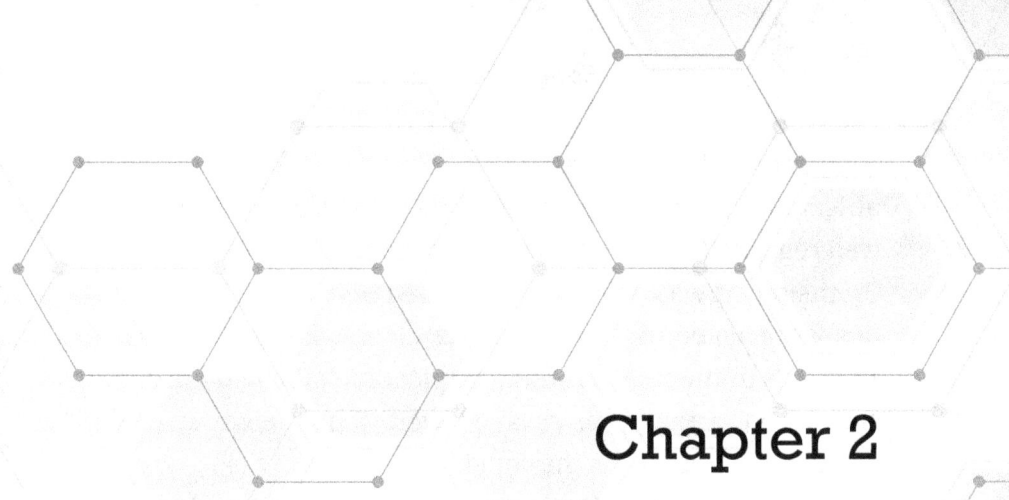

Chapter 2

Decisions for revival
Casually, and in depth
Not worthy for dismissal
But, embraced and kept

Mota's demeanor became less and less charming around her husband. With sleepless nights becoming more prevalent in her being, she aimed to improve her state of mind, through planning.

After Roi left for work, on a sunny morning, she stayed at her desk, on her planning calendar to carefully understand what she wanted to do. Despite a lockdown on communication with Roi, access to the kids prevention, and a separation of physical contacts in a 12-room house, Mota sensed such an arrangement would not work in the scheme of things. She sat at her desk, remembering the plagiarism case, in which Roi initially made her proud to be his wife, then without any warning shattered every fiber of her being. It began with his ethics committee involvement. A charge was being investigated at his firm, then was upgraded to an oversight by the ethics committee. Having been one of eight members in such a group, Roi was not totally satisfied with the initial outcome against one of the parties. He felt that there was a great deal of office politics favoring the guilty party. With his seniority and well regarded opinions, the process was stalled and restarted. On the day it was proven that Roi had been right, the two parties were asked to write on topics chosen by Roi, an essay of 75 words or more. At the end, the plagiarist seemed upset over such a request; and his essay proved to be the worst kind of writing imaginable. As the conclusion of such a task drew near, security had to be called to protect the innocent party, whose life would have been damaged beyond measure, without Roi's intervention. The plagiarist was fired by the committee, and reprimanded by Roi.

Mota remembered that day and was overjoyed by her husband's action in that particular case; but also remembered how surprised she was, when a dinner guest, two weeks later was the plagiarist, who had been fired and reprimanded.

From the notion of tolerance and criminal conspiracy, Mota felt extremely confused, and uneasy. After such a dinner, she could not help but ask.her husband's rationale for inviting a potentially criminally minded person into their lives, by leveling a personal platform to get to know him. His responses were vague and reprehensible. She never understood his mindset concerning this incident, as well as several others.

In the process of her planning strategies, Mota was still working on her planner, seated at her computer, typing away. She took notes, and had her list of pros and cons concerning her plans. The pros doubled in size. She took into consideration all of her conversations with Sti. She wondered how Sti would have reacted had she delved into details of instances of failure on the part of Roi. She never dared; since her psychoanalysis of Sti's mentality was proned to be wrapped around stability, and lack of compassion relative to things deemed unimportant. In other words, the essence of life should not be rocked, in instances where all of the necessities have been met, from Sti's point of view.

From her perspective, after 18 years, Mota felt that she deserved to be mentally free, and able to express her viewpoints. She sat there remembering the time one of Roi's friends stayed overnight, after asking a favor from Roi, to provide an alibi that he had been with him the entire evening; when in reality, this man had reached the house in the middle of the night. After spending a romantic evening with a mistress, this man feared reaching home during the wee hours of the morning. Mota, particularly recalled the phone calls from this man's wife, requesting that she speak to him, when he was not there yet. Roi, seemed overjoyed fibbing about this man's whereabouts in the house, when he wasn't even there.

Upon experiencing such a trauma from his demeanor and fibs, Mota, at that point, somewhat lost some respect for her husband. She had never expressed her emotions to him, during the days that followed. But, her notion of marital partnership seemed to evaporate into thin air.

Even a discussion on a landmark case (Roe v Wade) that legalizes abortion, startled Mota to a degree of awe in a negative sense. *"First of all, a 7-2 opinion doesn't sound right, in this country. I don't care what you think you believe is right, as far as I am concerned, the state of this case will never fully resolve..."blah, blah, blah..."* Mota recalled this very statement from her husband, an educated man whose philosophical views impressed her a great deal during courtship. She surmised that during the aging process, Roi's mentality became more and more combative regarding all aspects of life, and perhaps demanded challenging responses to debate more and more. While recalling this instance, she put into perspective the rationale for the discussion in the first place. They were having an exchange about their daughters. As the topic of pregnancy was filtering through in the conversation, Roi *commented* on the facts surrounding the reasons for abortions and teen pregnancy, being poor parenting, no other reason. Somewhere in the conversation, Mota felt offended that he suggested if any of their girls became impregnated, he would ensure that they would not have any other choice, but, to give birth.

The notion of such a predisposition terrified Mota, to the point of questioning him endlessly about his pro-life views and opinions on life as a whole.

From a philosophical viewpoint, people are divided on matters of pro-choice, and pro-life due to a myriad of issues that are debatable. For the purpose of writing this story, it can be said that in life, what guides us is a priority on what matters. Good fortune is reachable through different arrays of thinking. Some emotional riches are reached with the birth of a child; Others are fulfilled emotionally with the idea of retaining a choice, because, such a choice provides the underlying effects of the human factor. Can we, as members of society question a supreme opinion?

What lay on Roi's mind is the unfathomable notion of just ideas that ultimately guide him as a father, husband, and a human being.

The instance of the discussion stayed on Mota's mind, with some compassion dealing with the acceptance of differences in opinions. But, she condemned his comments relative to why there was higher involvement in such matters.

To make matters worse, her memory relative to his stance on immigrants, felt even more terrifying. While sitting at her desk, recalling these instances, she became hysterical, laughing, and maintaining her composure at the same time.

She thought *"How does an immigrant refer to other immigrants as being unworthy of an education?he has European blood, comingled with Caribbean blood, one of the typical common mixtures that are widespread all over...perhaps he just wanted to get under my skin..."*

She began to realize that a full separation had to occur to fully regain her normalcy of mind, body and spirit. But, how?

She continued typing plan A, starting with lodging, expenses, leisure activities, and essentials. As she typed, and typed, she thought about a favor from Sti which would prove to be extraordinary from a family friend of so many years, close to 17 to be exact. She knew the challenges that she would have to face with questions upon questions that would not be answered to Sti's liking. She also knew, as a friend, she would render an unbiased conclusion to the mental uneasiness she was facing as a wife and mother. As she began to make a phone call, sitting there, her daughter, Tori walked in to simply chat.

Meanwhile, Sino was walking around in her area, after school, pondering about psalm 56:3 on fear and trust "When I am afraid, I will put my trust in you" The remembrance of this scripture stemmed from a lack of certainty about her future family relationships. She knew her parents loved each other, but somehow, certain strains surfaced, making it difficult for them to have civilized conversations. Her father's off the wall comments penetrated her mind, as she recalled his philosophical stance–*"Sino,...do you realize that criminals contribute to the economy"..."how so, Dad?"*

"well, you see, bailbondsmen have mortgages, prison personnel have bills to pay, judges enjoy a busy schedule, and everyone else who is attached to the criminal justice system has to have a life."

"hmm,...well dad, I disagree with your position, but, the con-cept of law and order helps society function with peace of mind... if crimes were much less than they are today, the body of laws would have better oversight..., anyway, that is my opinion."

As she remembered, she smiled, asking herself if her father was real, when he made his remarks, without any type of warning.

Overall, from Mota's perspective, her choice of leaving, whether permanently or temporarily, had been made. Her daughters, with their distinct personalities agreed that a change had to occur. Culturally, as a multiracial family, their issues were somewhat atypical, particularly to Sti, whose friendship was held in high regard.

On her phone call to Sti, she left a message on her voicemail box. "Hi there, I need a favor, please call me back ASAP. Thanks"

In a parental arena, from which there can be a teachable moment, it's essential that the degree of severity of the circum-stances faced be understood by those involved. The responses from Mota's daughters, clearly signified a need for a change to proceed with their lives. On her journey, this woman taught her children on the importance attached to "trust"; and when it became crucial to communicate a disappointment.

Aside from a $35,000 bonus that was kept totally from her knowledge, other things became pronounced as she pondered about her married life.

What had she done to correct her situation? Both she and Roi, had attended marriage counseling, numerous times. The results had always favored Roi. *"your husband suffers from an acute illness called...extremely happily married"*or *"He has a sense of humor that is borderline combative...please don't take him seriously"*or *"a few days, weeks, apart can result in the affir-mation you're looking for"*...

The remarks from these counselors permeated on her mind; but instead of affirming strength to stay, she vowed she would stay away to understand her feelings, and why she sensed a voracious idea filtering through every time she attempted to analyze his psyche.

As Tori walked in to chat with her mother, after a long day of academia, she mentioned, right before her mother picked up the phone, that she wanted to discuss a poem that was written by one of Sino's bible study colleagues. With so much on Mota's mind, she acknowledged her daughter's presence with a nod and a smile, then continued to make notes about her plans.

The phone, then rang. It was Sti. "What's happening? I got your message"

"I made a decision to leave, for a while"

"What? No way...what happened?"

"You know how I've been feeling about my marriage...I just can't take it, right now"

"I know from what you've mentioned, that Roi can be very difficult...but..."

Interrupting Sti, Mota went on to say "Do you realize how much I've put up with his B.S..? well, do you?He kept something very important from me...he received a bonus from his firm of $35,000, and never revealed this."

"What? Why would he do such a thing? Did you ask him why he would do so?

"His answer was not an answer. It was a shrug"

"I understand your position. But, I need to tell you that you're one of the lucky ones"

"Lucky?"

"Yes, lucky. I have friends who find their husbands passed out on their floors, from a night of heavy drinking. I have others who can't invite anyone over for fear of embarrassment, and so many others with severe problems. I just hope you know what you're doing"

"I know what I am doing. I need a favor though"

"Anything, tell me..."

"I need you to report anything that he does while we're away. I mean anything and everything. What is revealed will determine whether or not I'll come back here."

"Mota, wait a minute, so I will be the deciding factor on the redemption of your marriage?that doesn't sound fair.does it?"

"I am sorry. But, you've been one of my best friends over several years. I will trust what you're able to surmise on anything"

"I will be biased, though, because I want you to save your marriage. I mean...I know he is a decent man, with a twisted mentality; but, he is not too bad, from my perspective. I may not be the best person to do this for you, Mota. I am sorry"

"I will not be too far away. But, I will need someone to report to me about his whereabouts"

"I understand your need to escape from within. As unfortunate as it may seem, such a quest may be the right medicine for this relationship"

"Thank you for expressing how you feel. That's one of the reasons why I trust and respect you"

"So, when exactly will you be leaving?"

"Day after tomorrow"

"Does he know what you're doing?"

A click on the phone was heard by both of them.

Sti probed into it and said: "What was that"?

"Do I really need to tell you who was listening to this conversation"

"Do you mean, Roi was listening?"

"Sino and Biamu are not here. Tori is standing right here..."

"I simply don't know what to say. Sometimes, certain things are necessary"

"Precisely"

"Ok. So, be well, and keep in touch. "

"I will. Bye for now"

Sti hung up on her end, and felt dumbfounded.

Sti stood for a few minutes in her home office, trying to remember Roi's interactions with her. *"He seemed jovial, every time I went over for dinner with my son...Always so cheerful, but, full of "off the wall"remarks. I remember the time he mentioned that the difference between regular and premium gas being the same as the difference between tap water and bottled water...; and then, made a switch, that he preferred tap water. I remember thinking, where is the message in this?but, his remarks never bothered me.."*

Sti then began to understand the position she was in. Then, she immediately called Mota and told her to read the book of James. 3:2 "For we all stumble in many ways. And, if anyone does not stumble in what he says, he is a perfect man, able also to bridle his whole body" She also asked her to reconsider her options.

Mota declined to discuss her situation further and told her she would keep in touch.

Chapter 3

New environment grasped
Strategizing with fervor
Absorbing the plan, wrapped
Approaching things with candor

The world seemed different to Mota in so many ways. In a new environment, with her 3 daughters, she felt different. Not too Far away from her house, her new location offered somewhat the same convenience and luxury, except for familiarity of her norm. The seasonal home was of the same size, within the same county, and school district. Her daughters did not change school; nor did they reach out to new friends.

Prior to leaving her husband, she left a note, explaining her rationale for deciding to part ways *"if not permanently,.it will be temporary..."* She explained that it was necessary to proceed with her plans, since, even though they separated while under the same roof, there was no change of behavior on his part. She also explained the rage that she felt about a hidden bonus of $35,000, which she felt she had the right to know about.

Roi, upon reading the note, sat on the couch, and looked into space for a while, scratching his head, and grinning.

The girls, on the other hand, supported their mom, 100%. With the type of philosophy upon which they were raised, not in a million years, would they not admonish their father's ideas, and potentially awful influence on their lives. Although supportive, they made it clear to their mom, that they indeed, loved their father. They simply disagreed with his ways.

With the luxury and convenience of working from home or offsite, Mota continued with her work, to support herself and her daughters. Since there was no divorce, no actual, or official arrangements were made with respect to finances.

Her last communication with Roi was brief; and stipulated that her action of leaving may be temporary, since she needed to understand herself more than anything else. He nodded at that time, kissed her forehead, after handing her a small luggage, filled with mementos.

From Mota's viewpoint, his act of handing her pieces of items they had both collected at their vacation spots, was meant to allow her to remember good times on their outings. She did take time to absorb what had become of their marriage.

Her girls kept busy with their schedules, in school and in their respective sports activities. On one particular day, Tori requested assistance with translation of a French poem, Sino had handed her. The poem, written by one of Sino's bible study colleagues, seemed complexed and filled with hidden meanings. As such, Sino wanted to leave an impression of comprehension to her class. She enlisted the aid of Tori, who had been well versed in the "French"language.

Tori left a copy of the poem with her mom, as she walked out to report to school. Before she left, she simply placed the copy on Mota's desk, saying: "I need help with this, mom. Sino wants to decipher what's going on in her friend's life. Let me know if you understand it, and please give me some input"

Before even responding to her request, while sitting in her new home office, she nodded, and waved, with the intention of looking at it eventually.

In a process of absorbing it all; managing the situation and placing some form of normalcy with the daily routines, at times, a neglect can seep through.

Mota became more and more concerned about certain aspects of her new life; while neglecting some other aspects.

Putting aside her analysis of the poem, she maintained some focus in the work she felt committed to. At times, she turned back to the poem to re-read and re-analyze. The poem reads:

"Il n'est pas suffisant?..."

Vie de terreur, et de malheur
Existence de persistence et de foi
Malgre les sentiments des heures
Continue avec un Espoir de droit

Les parties privées
Entourées par les effets d'un courant
Sont tout de meme affectées
Mais, sans doute, protegées par le sang

Le sang du Seigneur, Jesus Christ
Versé pour tous, sur la croix
Symbolique, et necessaire par un cri
Le cri de ses adversaires, tant de fois

Une vie de substance
Tout le monde la possede, et retient

Une difference de traitement danse
Toujours et partout, revient

Changements qui se presentent
Peuvent etre chaleureux et de bon gré
Les marques, continuant, froissantes
Aident à maintenir mentalite à clé

Le Bon Dieu protège tous
Tous qui ont besoin de sa protection
En lui demandant avec foi, en tout
Les demandes sacrées de direction

Toutes ces années, en froid
Chansons d'Aznavour
Filtrations de simple joie
Permettant les motions verbales, en tour

Perte d'emploi gagnant
Devrait etre suffisante
D'autres pertes enormes, comptant
Sans jugement et realization, justifiant

Mota attempted to decipher each stanza with a great deal of insights into a very darkened, emotional place of which the writer was expressing her innermost feelings. She analyzed in writing each part of the document, with the intention of remitting it to Tori when she returned from school.

The process of providing some type of input in any situation requires a keen sense of the whole picture. Although she was not able to ascertain the whole picture and sense of involvement in any particular interests, she was able to surmise that this person needed some type of emotional assistance.

Upon completing her written analysis, based on her knowledge of the French language, she set it aside. As she continued to work on her own duties, her phone rang. Sti wanted to know how things had been working out; and also wanted to relay that all seemed quite normal from Roi's end. She explained that she ensured that the property was kept in good appearance, through chatting with the gardener, at times. Mota chatted with her for a while, then thanked her for keeping her apprised of things, since it had already been a couple of months since she left.

On that very day, when Biamu walked in, she conversed with her mom about her day, and mentioned the fact that she had overheard a conversation between a few people. "What did you overhear?"

"A man sat by the downtown waterfall, to somehow preach or guide a few people. I overheard him say how certain turnarounds in life begin after three incidents occur...what do you think that means?"

"Wow, I am not sure...try not to pay attention to people's conversations next time.you know better than that."

"But, I couldn't help it. It felt like he was talking to me..."

"How can that be? Have you ever seen him before?"

"No. It's just that, I miss Dad, a little. Sometimes I think there ought to be a way to mend this family; and when he said that, I paid attention."

"We promised we would not talk about the situation between your father and me. Remember that?"

"Yes...I just wanted to tell you about my day..."

Sadly, Mota sensed certain tensions and wished for the first time, since leaving that she had made it clearer why she had decided to leave.

Shortly thereafter, Sino walked in, waved to her mom and went to her room. An apparent conversation with Biamu and Sino ensued.

With her knowledge of biblical scripture, Sino explained her points of view relative to the possible significance of the conversation overheard.

"...I am not 100% certain of what he may have been talking about. But, I know for sure that the number three. At times, can be a positively significant number biblically"

"Do you feel that mom and Dad will eventually get back together"

"I have no idea. Based on what I've read in the bible, many things happened three times. For instance, in Matthew 4:1-11, Jesus' ministry lasted three years. In Luke 22:54-62, Peter denied him three times. In John, 21:15-17, he affirmed his love for humanity three times. There are several other meanings attached to three. There is a belief, that some negativity is attached to it – like: Satan, Anti-Christ, and false prophecy. But, overall, it may be a positive thing that the man was talking about..."

"I understand. I sometimes have a real icky feeling about everything"

"You need to stop worrying. Have you chosen your college and law school yet?"

"I think after high school, I'll take a year off, to decide"

"You know, mom will not agree to that"

Their conversation was lengthy; exchanging back and forth opinions and ideas about different topics. Most importantly,

Biamu left a very essential aspect of her day out of the conversation.

While she sat by the waterfall, an extremely good looking young man, walked up to her. Without any conversation whatsoever, he planted a kiss on her left cheek. She looked up and noticed his eyes, as he smiled and slowly walked away.

Shortly thereafter, is when the conversation was overheard.

In essence, biblically, we learn typically about the Trinity, (Father, Son and the Holy Spirit), relative to spiritual beliefs. As it is written in the bible, we answer for our lives to a divine account, in the form of three spiritual beings in one. The significance of this number lies in the number of times it is repeated – four hundred sixty seven times, in biblical scripture. Worth mentioning are the facts that three visitors appeared to Abraham, Gen. 18:2; Noah had three sons, Gen. 6:10; Jonah was inside of the belly of a fish for three days, Jonah 1:17.

Overhearing a conversation may have been meaningful from Biamu's perspective, because of the developments in her home life; and the fact that she wished things had been different.

From the development of the story, if there were to be three incidents that could identify the specific weaknesses in Mota's marriage, at least one has been noted.

Being approached by a stranger, and receiving warmth in the form of a kiss on the left cheek, is not considered the norm. Such an incident can potentially be one of the incidents that can be counted toward a fulfilling end.

Chapter 4

Startling observations
Despair, for an instant
Grasping mental dictations
Striving from being distant

Sti knelt down at her church, praying for guidance and strength as an enormous burden is felt to have been placed on her shoulders. She looked around as she prayed, hoping for some signs of a response to her demands. She prayed: "*Lord, as your servant, I need to understand the fullness of this task that I am supposed to supervise. I spoke to my friend, Mota, several times, and was unable to tell her the full impact of what I've seen. Although it may not mean much, I find it difficult to express to her, in all honesty, what I saw on her driveway, without placing some type of judgment. I know I need to investigate further, before concluding anything. Because I know her husband would not be that foolish to involve himself in anything that would further jeopardize his marriage. He can be slightly immature, but, this...No, I can't think of any positive about this. But, I need your help in guiding me on how to approach this situation...*" Her prayer continued in the same line of thoughts. She continued to look around in the almost totally empty church, with just around eight parishioners sitting with their rosaries. She sat down and continued to pray.

Two days prior, she drove on Mota's block, and noticed a young woman washing her car in the driveway. She thought: *"Wait a minute, that's Mota's driveway...what's going on, here?Let me turn around, and take a closer look."* She turned around; and there it was. A young hippie looking thirtyish woman was washing her car. Without any inclination as to who this woman was, and what the relationship to Roi, she represented, Sti began to make slight logical judgment. Her heart was beating extremely fast, and didn't know how she would make such a revelation to Mota.

As she sat at the church, silently praying, she noticed an older gentleman, holding a girl's hand, directing her to sit next to him—a fatherly figure that appeared totally normal. From her standpoint, seeing such a scenery was somewhat of a sign from God, pointing out to her, that the situation may have been a guarding type arrangement. The lump in her throat somewhat decreased in size; and her feelings of uneasiness, lessened. She sat there for another few minutes, then left.

At the house, all seemed normal. Tori appeared to decipher the meaning of the poem which had been translated by her mom. Hoping to provide input to Sino, whose friendship with this person, continued to grow, she intended to discuss the whole meaningful aspects of the writing.

Tori sat down on her bed to read her mom's analysis:

"Dear Tori, I am not sure what the real meaning of this poem is but, here is my take on it: This writer is talking about "life"being terror filled, and living life based on faith. Although the hours of the day are not very good, life continues with the spirit of human rights. Private parts...(I am not understanding this aspect) are protected by the blood of Christ, spilled for all,

symbolizing a necessity and his sacrifice because of the demands of his adversaries. Life can be of substance for everyone, but a disparity in treatment continues to linger. Changes are good. But, the mistrust is still there, and perhaps diminishing. The Lord protects all who requests protection. All they should do is ask for direction. All these years in the cold. But, Aznavour music kept her verbal skills operational. Loss of gainful employment should have been enough. But, apparently, other major losses occurred. No real justifiable judgment took place" If you can add anything else, please let me know.

Tori read it and jotted some notes to present to Sino, who initially requested assistance in translation. At that point, she surmised that her sister was engaged in important work to uplift, and perhaps even counsel her bible study group.

With the hope of providing significant input to this cause, Tori summarized what she thought she could infiltrate into the meaning, and had her own opinions along the same lines as her mother's translations.

Meanwhile, Sti sat in her home office, emailing members of her club on upcoming events. One of her particular interests was ground maintenance. Any visuals that were not to her liking around the grounds, received extreme criticisms aimed at the ground keepers, and managers. Her role was to ensure that the area was kept in the utmost perfection. As hard as she had been working, on and off, she found some time to analyze the situation dealing with Mota's issues. She made it a point to plan on her next movement regarding her investigative quest. Such a quest dealt with Roi, and an apparent guest, that she felt somewhat uneasy about. She finished her last email message; closed down her laptop; took her keys and wallet, and headed out.

She drove down her neighborhood, made a left turn toward Mota's house. She stopped across from there, and noticed the gardener doing his work. She stepped out of her car and walked straight to the gardener. "Hi, sorry to bother you. But, I was wondering about something."

"Ma'am?"

"I am sorry ..."She looked at the gardener and realized she had not introduced herself, but started speaking as if they had talked before.

"So sorry."she said; and continued. "I am a friend of Mota's, Mrs. Turot's...and I noticed that you've been the gardener for her house."

"Yes, ma'am...I've been gardening for the past few years... how can I help you?"

"As you may know, Mrs. Turot has not been home, for a while now..."

"Yes, ma'am."

"There was a car here, the other day. I've never seen it before...do you know anything about any new guests who may have arrived here?"

"I know that Mr. Turot is hardly here. He pays me for the entire summer, and tells me I am on my own, and that he trusts me. As far as guests..., I am not sure who and what you mean."

"Let me be blunt. There was a young lady, the other day, wearing a flimsy attire. She was washing her car on the driveway. Have you any idea who she might be?"

"No ma'am."

"Let me give you my number. I want you to call me if you see or hear anything. I will make it worth your while. I am just a caring friend."

"I understand."

"I need to know who she is, and what she is doing here."Her voice was shaky and appeared to lose vocality.

The gardener took the number, and seemed equally concerned because of Sti's demeanor; then said: "ok, I'll see what I can find out for you, ma'am"

"Thank you. I appreciate it. By the way, was she here today?"

"I did see a young lady outside, smoking a cigarette, earlier today."

"I thank you for taking my number; and please give me a call as soon as you can tell me anything"

"Yes, ma'am, I will."

Sti felt accomplished, with her investigative efforts. She walked toward her car; got in, then drove off.

"So, she was there today. I have to know what's going on, before I alert Mota on anything. I am opining that it's nothing. But, I need facts. Roi would be out of his mind, if he picked up some hussy from the streets and bring her there..."

A good friend that Sti had turned out to be, considering that at the inception of meeting Mota, the sparks of friendship were hardly there. On her way home, from talking to the gardener, her thoughts on what, and how she would respond to the challenges of knowing what she knew, which was basically not much, were wavering in her head.

For the rest of the day, she stayed home, to look over her planner, respond to email messages, and basically surfed the Web. After a few hours, close to sleeping time, her cell phone rang.

"Hello"She picked up.

"Ma'am, we spoke earlier today..."

"Yes, tell me. What is it?"With trembling hands, she waited for a reply.

"I don't know if this is anything. But, before I left a few moments ago, the lady that you asked about, was talking to Mr. Turot; and both were talking to an older gentleman"

"I don't understand. Did they seem together, talking to this person?"

"From what I can tell, the lady seems to be with the gentleman, but not with Mr. Turot."

"Are you saying that this person..."

"I think her name is Bromar..."

"Are you saying this Bromar person appears to be with this man, together, as guests at Mrs. Turot's house?"

"I think so. I've seen this man before. It's Mr. Martin."

"Can you, actually, feel that there's anything wrong with the picture"

"No ma'am. I don't know what you mean. But, from what I can see, this lady came with Mr. Martin, to visit Mr. Turot."

"Thank you for your opinion on this. I will stop by soon, to compensate you for your time. So, are you saying I should not be suspicious about this young woman?"

"I understand how you feel, being a friend of Mrs. Turot, and all.., but, I reckon that nothing seems to be suspicious..."

"I thank you again. I will compensate you. Good Bye, and thank you, again"

Sti held on to her cell phone, and chuckled a little. "*So, this girl, Bromar young woman, is probably visiting, along with someone else. I think I feel better. But, now I feel more comfortable paying Roi a visit, to confirm everything about this visit...*"

With thoughts, swirling all over the place, Sti felt so much better about the whole notion that certain suspicions should be dissipated. She was glad to have presented her dilemma to a higher power. While sitting at that church, it became clear to her what she had been dealing with was far less severe than originally thought. She thought of 1 Corinthians 4:5 "Therefore, form no premature judgments, but wait..." That, she did.

Although she felt totally at ease. She decided to drive over just to confirm that the gardener had revealed the truth. When she reached Mota's place, she noticed Roi's car, as well as the car she had seen before, on the driveway. Lights were on. She figured that his guests had stayed over, a few days. *"But, why?*she thought.

At that point, she surmised that it would be safe to mention her efforts to Mota.

Sino, who for several biblical conferences, was named group leader, felt very busy, doing her task of leading her group. She developed a great deal of self confidence, dealing and advising with caution what she needed to. One member of her group was a competitor, challenging every word she uttered, and coming up with a different solution to every challenge. She maintained her ground on every topic, without insulting the challenger on her disrespect. As a matter of fact, as she learned more about the word, she became more and more understanding of others based on human nature. Sino was simply very mature for her age.

During one of her conferences, an extremely good looking fellow walked in. She welcomed him and asked whether or not he wanted to join the bible study group. He answered in the affirmative; and was asked to sit with the other members. Throughout the conference, this young man did nothing but stare at her without seemingly knowing how uncomfortable he made her feel. She talked about "Revelation, the book of James, and 2nd Chronicles" With input from the members, she was able to complete her conference as intended. Upon finishing, she wondered why he seemed so different. His eyes were intrusive in a very pleasant way; and he seemed to wear a smile that was somewhat contagious. The end of the night could not come soon enough. She felt very strange and somewhat shy. Although she seemed totally in control of her group, somehow, his presence left a lasting impression on her whole being. After the last member bid her Good Bye, the stranger stood up, and asked: "Do you go out at all?"

"I am not sure what you're asking."

"I like you. I think you're doing a great job, here."

"Thank you"

"You haven't answered my question."

"To answer you, no. I am not interested. Thank you for coming here, today."

"Oh, what's wrong? Maybe in the future?"

"I am not sure"

"Your name is Sino, right?"

"Right."

"All right, well, you know, perhaps it is not the right time to ask you out. May I ask again, tomorrow?"

"We don't have a conference, tomorrow. I am sorry"

"So, you're leaving me out in the cold, like this?"

"I need to leave, right now. Thank you, for coming"

"Next time, I'll wear a better shirt"

"Good Bye"

"You haven't even asked me for my name"

"I guess you'll tell us all next time, won't you?"

"I suppose...Ok. So, I'll see you next time"

"Bye...I'll give you a bible, if you don't have one"

"I do have one. I'll bring it with me"

"Thank you"

Sino took her belongings, and walked the other way, in the church through a side door. She thought about the strange conversation, and felt a little tingly. She smiled, and giggled on her way to her car. The stranger walked out of another door.

Mota, just like most mothers embraced the social norm of virtue relative to marital bliss. Her daughters' inclination was directed toward this norm, with slight deviation limited to imagination and fantasy. Sino, on her way home, that day, felt a certain sense of arrival as it relates to holding feelings of romance, and possibilities. She was smiling as she drove, wondering if any of her sentiments were real with this stranger who actually came out of nowhere. *"He seemed pretty funny"*... she thought, as she smiled all the way home.

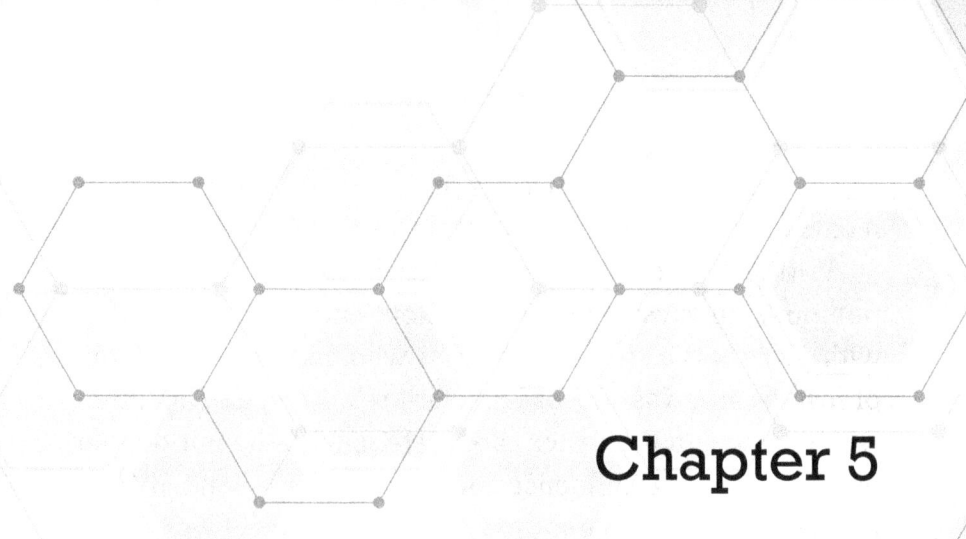

Chapter 5

Nurturing close bonds
To keep and to treasure
Disregarding in emotional ponds
And proceed with pleasure

Lars became very close to Arias, since they were in the same school for at least 3 years. Arias was adopted by Mota's sister, after attempting to rob her. With the goodness of her heart, Tam was elated to have had a chance to adopt a son. In one of her outings to Mota's house, Arias brought along Lars as a party buddy, four years prior. Since then, Lars had grown mature, and had become somewhat of a "catch", by most standards. Although both of these young men were tall, dark and handsome, Lars' presence arose much more attention.

Both Sino and Biamu had absolutely no idea that somehow, this young man was somewhat lurking, to solicit interests. At the time of the party to which both girls were simply not interested in romance or anything remotely at that level, it was a non-incident, from their perspective.

Arias, on the other hand, had always considered these girls as "family" Even though they weren't blood related, his gratitude for having a home, an adoptive mom who loved him, and an opportunity to enhance his life, prevailed over any sentiments of non-brotherly, or cousinly love.

With extremely good looks, Lars became conceited, and pompous, always ready for the next catch. His friendship with Arias was a special one. Arias who had been in and out of foster care, was one of Lars' father's projects. The father who engaged in the foster care system, with the notion that only surroundings influenced one's character, defended Arias for every bad deed committed.

Eventually, when Mota's sister adopted him, it was through Lars' father that such was accomplished.

It appears that in life, the most important endeavor is to keep, and maintain the bare necessities; e.g, a roof over one's head, the daily bread, proper hygienic tools, proper guidance, and most importantly, a relationship with God. Prior to being part of a foster care system, some may not have had the nurturing needed to transform into what's socially acceptable, but, with the possibility of finding what's needed in such a system, the idea of hope travels.

Lars was ready to attend another bible study conference, which was to be presided over by Sino.

On Roi's front, all seemed optimistic. He never once doubted that his wife would not return. During the early morning hours, as he engaged in preparing for a work meeting, his bell rang. Sti who had the utmost interest of Mota's at heart, wanted to ensure that all was well on Roi's front. She drove and parked her car right across from Mota's place, and waited a few minutes before actually exiting the car. She walked up, and noticed the same automobile she had questioned earlier in the week, and received some sort of explanation. She also noticed Roi's car parked next to it on the driveway.

Chapter 5

After ringing the bell, she waited at the door. The door opened. Roi, with a serious look on his face greeted her. "Sti, what brings you here, today?"Sti cleared her throat, and said "Hi, I was in the neighborhood, and decided to drop by to see my good friend's husband and find out how he is doing..., may I come in?

"Of course,...silly me, blocking you like this...yes, please come in."

"I have been so busy with work, that I don't even miss the kids, anymore.., can I offer you anything to gulp down?"

"No, Roi, I don't need to gulp anything down. I noticed a strange car; and I felt it was perhaps a long time friend who came for a visit.., ?

"...Oh, yeah, Bromar is on drugs. She is such a disrespectful little thing..., she is here with her father Martin..."

"Martin is a friend of yours..., Ok, I understand. What are they doing here, if you don't mind my asking?"

"Do you really want to know, Sti? His daughter has given him so much strife in his life with his new wife, that he just had to get away for a few days...like I said, she can be one troublesome young lady..."

As Sti listened to Roi, she became more at ease with the situation, assessing that indeed the gardener had given her good information. She also had to stop listening, when Bromar simply walked through the living room without any sign of respect. Her attire, represented her mentality from head to toe. She didn't say hello, or excuse me for walking through. Her demeanor was that of a young lady with serious inner feelings issues. She passed them, through the living room to reach the kitchen, then sat legs wide open on the middle island, after fetching an edible from the freezer. Her back was to them; so the bodily offense was somewhat minimized. Without any regard on whether or not she might hear the conversation, Roi exclaimed to Sti...".…This is the type of demeanor I never want to experience with my girls. Mart has tried desperately to fix this, but I am afraid he'll never garner enough strength to do it...it simply cannot be done."

"I understand...but, why are they here?does Mota approve of this?

"Mota left. All decisions that I make concerning my way of life, are based on my intuition alone. She gave up on our marriage to seek herself; and frankly, I hope she's found what she had been seeking..."

"It's only temporary, Roi. She hasn't left...She will be back...I am sure of it."

"I know. I haven't sold the house; and frankly, sometimes, I think about it. I simply don't know how long she needs to decide what her life should be."

"If you don't mind my asking, what about the $35,000 that you failed to disclose to her...what was that about?"

"Sti,...you don't want to go there. It's a long story...talking about it will be useless...Really."

"I just want to offer my friendship fully. The two of you belong together. I simply don't want to see this ended unnecessarily. She asks about you, every time I call her. Just wanted to let you know..."

"...Mota is an emotional woman. One of the reasons why I married her. She was very sentimental and sensitive that I knew the rest of my life belonged to her. But, out of the blue, she wanted to step out...temporarily, or not, it's hard to accept sometimes..."

"I realize that you two probably needed time to get reacquainted. It's common in certain marriages..."

Chapter 5

Roi stood up with his hands in his pocket, while looking over at his desk..."Are you sure I can't offer you anything?"

Sti knew it was time to leave; and said..."No, I have a lot on my plate too, today."

She said goodbye. As she stepped toward the door, Martin was walking down the steps, ...sleepily saying..."Why didn't you wake me up..."? Addressing Roi with this question, didn't seem out of the ordinary from Sti's standpoint. She continued to walk toward the door, and left.

As Roi returned to his home office, his mind was racing wondering how he would handle Bromar's disrespect. He then remembered the question. He answered with a wave of his left hand–"unless there was a good reason to have awakened you, ...oh, by the way, your daughter was most disrespectful a little while ago. I have an idea on how to fix this issue..."

"...What else is new ?"Martin walked to the kitchen, mumbling..."...*What can I do to change things with this girl. First she threatened to harm my wife..., then she got suspended from school, several times, I bailed her out from the slammer for driving drunk with a bunch of friends..., now that I am here temporarily to cool things off, she's being mean to Roi?what am I going to do, with this woman, young woman? Counseling doesn't help..., what am I going to do? I have to go back home soon..., I can't stay here forever...what am I going to do?*"

Martin fit the role of a good father, wanting to protect his child, at the same time, unable to fix the mental troubles that were tormenting her.

Philippians 2:4 "Let each of you look not only to his own, but, also to the interests of others"

From this scripture, it seems clear that Roi's intents on addressing Bromar's issues represented a gesture that would somehow aid Martin's efforts in disciplining his daughter.

At the same time, Roi was working very intensely on a case involving a colleague who had been terminated from his company for years. Following the termination, not only was this colleague provided no severance, she was blacklisted, and slandered to her family and friends. The case involved heresays from one source. After all the years that elapsed, and finding no real path to regain her footing, Roi got involved through the company's requests. Roi devised a plan to get to the truth. He communicated directly with the source of this woman's problems; and effectuated a plan for an open hearing. He advised the source, to provide written documents, under oath, so that if any revelations were found to be false, they would be held accountable and possibly punished based on federal laws. Within days, the source began to change its position, thereby leaving Roi no choice but to suggest reparations for this woman's life, after her life had been damaged severely.

From such an outcome, it is clear that, given enough tolerance to one group of people, whose motivation is to witness the degradation of people they dislike, no mercy would ever be recognized or granted, from their viewpoints. Had it not been for the threat of prosecution, this source would have continued with continuous lies, and made up falsehoods to hurt this woman.

Roi's summation of his analysis comprised of different types of psychological viewpoints; ranging for fear of intimidation, to unwanted accountability. At times, when an erroEonus judgment is made against someone, whose life has been greatly affected by such judgment, the presiding authority of such, may or may not feel any responsibility. Those, in reality, who would feel the brunt of responsibility, may feel self diminished, and lose, their self respect in the process. Nevertheless, it is important to understand that perfection does not exist in humanity. People err, today; have erred yesterday; and will err tomorrow. The most important thing to remember relates to immediate correction when clarity is received, relative to injustice. The indifference that occurs, when the truth is known, especially if an act of adulation is possible, can create a catalyst for adversity. As a well respected member of his firm, his analysis was read, acted upon, and felt highly regarded.

On the home front, Roi devised different ways to deal with Bromar's disrespectful attitude. His plan to lessen the impact of her disrespect was beginning to take shape.

Meanwhile, on the other side of town, Lars and Arias continued their friendship sharing thoughts on activities they engaged in. Their sports schedules were virtually the same, be it basketball, soccer, track and field, and swimming. Arias always enjoyed his visits with Lars, who was equipped with all sorts of technological gadgets. At times, he always wondered how his life would have been, had he had everything that Lars possessed. His life had been saved when he was a pre-teen; however, his thoughts on what could have been if he had his parents were a constant reminder of what he had lost.

His friendship with Lars amazed him to the point of awe. Lars had certain viewpoints that were startling, and unusual. He spoke as a prophet, quoting verses every chance he got; he talked about Moses, more often than not; he believed that a woman's place was in the home, and nowhere else; regulations to advance women's rights were felt to be useless by him. Arias, at times, would take the time to absorb what he said on several occasions, then found himself in agreement with him. But, as soon, as he began to attach some type of comprehension to issues discussed, he would change his position and rationalize as to why he felt the way he did. One particular issue involved his choice of one from many. Lars believed that he had the right to choose his mate from one family, dating one, or two at a time, to allow him to make a choice. Arias, on the other hand felt differently, particularly due to Lars' venturing to get to know Tori, after meeting Biamu and Sino. The real drama stemmed from the fact that none of the sisters knew what his game entailed.

Arias felt compelled to get involved, because of his closeness to his mom, who had been there for him from day one; even on the day he robbed her. He knew how much his mom, Tam, loved her sister, and her nieces. From his perspective, Lars would not intentionally hurt any of these girls; however, he surmised that his ideology would be traumatic to any girl who fell in love with him. Arias wasn't sure how to handle the situation; being that Lars had been adamant about seeking a relationship within the family unit, at any emotional cost. He decided that he would advise his mom of his suspicions. He felt determined to prove that Lars was the wrong man to date any of his adoptive cousins.

Chapter 6

Confusion, Intermingling with will
Deception, abound
Requests and desires that fill
An idea, a notion, sound

Proverbs 21:16 "It's better to live in the wilder-
ness, than to dwell with a contentious woman" The interpre-
tation of such a biblical scripture gears toward a choice for
peace over war.

Roi, as an upright man, from his perspective, elected to
understand that constant bickering was not going to be the
choice for his life. He became more and more oblivious to his
choice, as he was now having to deal with disrespect from a
young lady, with whom, he had absolutely no biological ties.
The love for his friend, Martin outweighed all feelings of indifference, to aid in the nurturing of this person. He became very
serious in attempting to elevate his cause in needing total
respect. His approach was unorthodox. However, it worked.

On the other side of town, Mota was on her daily run,
burning calories. As she jogged, she looked around her, being
careful, as usual. During her jogging, her cell phone was
silenced, but kept on "vibrate" She felt it vibrating. She didn't

answer but knew she would return the call as soon as she returned home. Her routine lasted for about one hour. When she reached her home, she stretched for a few more minutes, and ended her exercise routine.

She walked in; took out a bottle of Poland Springs, and reached for her cell phone to see who had called. It was Sti.

"Just checking up on you, and to give you an update. Call me back" The message was heard; and Mota was not ready to answer, or to call her back. But, she knew after her shower, she would do so.

Standing by her window, and feeling at home, with no emotional headaches, or concerns, Mota sipped her tea, wondering whether or not she would return to her previous life. A new-found freedom can be a pleasant experience, however if certain feelings outweigh such, it would be just a matter of time to pack it all in, and proceed with a decision. But, the time to do so, had not come yet.

She thought about her girls; how they had grown over the few months they had left. A change was perceived but, not analyzed. Sino had come home, later than expected, a couple of times. Biamu giggled more often than usual. Tori, on the other hand, became slightly more analytical than before. Her stance on understanding life as a whole was more pronounced.

All three of Mota's daughters involved themselves in several activities. Under the supervision of their mom, they maintained a stance of decency in terms of overall lifestyles. How they presented themselves in public; their hygiene upkeep; the deadline for chores assigned; the time they reported home from wherever, whether church or school or leisure activities; and the interaction mandated at dinner time, whenever it was possible–All of these standards were based on family obligations and norms.

Chapter 6

Sino sat at her desk in her room, rummaging through all sorts of papers. Some of these papers summarized different sets of situations gathered from some of the members, requesting aid from the church. As a member of her ministry, her bible study assignments were of the utmost importance. Her ministry work supplemented her school work and provided a significant meaning to her existence; and she loved it. One of the members who detailed her life story to Sino in a letter, caught her attention; as she was determined to help that woman.

She had already set a plan in motion, involving Arias, who gladly wanted to assist her in any way he could.

More importantly, Sino's mind was concentrated on Lars, who had left an impression on her that she simply could not ignore. She sat there, wondering what to do. She was specifically thinking about the night before, where after her meeting had concluded, Lars was there through the end, standing there, looking at her, with a smile. She felt somewhat uncomfortable, and asked exactly what he wanted. To which, he replied: "There are times when certain things are called for, and it's best to let things fall where they may."She was dumbfounded and simply shrugged off the remark. What shocked her was the fact that she had not reacted with anger or sarcasm, and she wondered why. When he approached her to let her know he liked her and wanted to court her as his girlfriend, Sino began to feel extremely uneasy, but, not angry or disgusted.

As she gathered her bible work, and ensuring all was placed back in order, he stood back with his arms crossed and glimpsed every now and then at what she was engaged in doing. When she was through, she simply said: "I am afraid it's time to exit. I have to leave now..., thank you for your interest..."

With a smile on her face, after he left the premises, her physical sensations, and her overall psyche, had somehow been perked up in a way that she had never experienced. She noticed him driving a Scion convertible, as he waited in the lot for her to leave before he did. She drove past him, and very slowly waved and drove off.

Sitting at her desk, reminiscing about the previous day, was an adventure. Startled by her cell ringing, she came back to her senses, and said "Hello"..

"Sino, I think I know exactly how to do this. I want to speak to her ex-husband, point blank, and get info right from his mouth, and maybe, He might understand that what he is doing is wrong, if it's really him."

"Well, be careful. Some people don't like to be confronted that way. Are you going to introduce yourself?"

"I want to engage in a conversation, first. Actually, I think I know where he hangs out..., I'll keep in touch."

"Arias, promise me that if you find out anything, that you will let me know right away"

"You got it, definitely, I've got this..."

"Ok, keep in touch"

"I will...All right, Bye."

Sino felt overjoyed; not because she expected a change in the life of this woman that she so desperately wanted to help; but because it certainly was a step in the right direction.

What stunned her particularly about this woman was the fact that there had been a massive conspiracy cornering her entire being. Rebuilding her life could not happen. Her ex hus-band's friends appeared to have a consortium to keep her from advancing in any spectrum of life. Even attempting to develop friendships, was challenging to the point of illegality. Sino understood somewhat what was probably happening; but, because of her level of maturity, she could not grasp the possibility of political involvement; special interest groups; the need to control mind and body; and the downright disregard for human rights. She, however, was smart enough to understand that what the woman had described to her, was simply unfair to the woman, as a human being.

Around the same time, Biamu was sitting by the waterfalls, hoping that Lars would keep his word. Two days prior, She sat at the same spot, reviewing notes on courtroom practices, as she was planning to attend college and decide on law school preference. She was simply relaxing and reading notes, and jotting her thoughts, as she felt someone sitting next to her. She glimpsed and her heart almost stopped working. Lars had a big smile, and he uttered that he didn't mean to startle her. "That's quite all right...I am not startled."as her heartbeats took a swing upward. She remembered this man kissing her on her cheek and could not understand the reason. They chatted a bit, along the lines of school, leisure activities, plans for the future and other petty but, important points. She felt more at ease as the conversation became more and more comfortable. After a couple of hours of talk, Biamu sensed certain feelings that she had never felt before. They ended the day, with Lars' remark: "let's meet here in a couple of days, at around the same time" She smiled. He kissed her on her left cheek, and waved goodbye.

True to his word, he showed up and took her by the hand, and said "Let's walk."

Arias, on his end, somewhat accomplished what he wanted to. He drove around for a while, and decided to stop by Lars' home to visit with him and chat about what he had attempted to do a few minutes prior.

His driver's license was brand new. He passed his test the month prior, and was promised a "smart car"if he passed. His mom surprised him with the gift of a brand new automobile. He felt blessed beyond measure. One of the many reasons why he cherished his adoptive family ties; and would do all that was asked of him, within reason, of course. So, as he parked his car, he kept thinking about what Lars had been up to. He walked up the steps, and was met with Lars' brother, Usam, (A Christ lookalike). Pleased to have seen Usam rather than lars relieved his stress, somewhat. "He is not here. I need to talk to him too. Are you here to shake him up, a bit?"

"No. I am here to just chat and see what he's doing"

"He is up to no Good, did you know that?"

"mmmm, I guess. But, can you tell me what you're thinking?"

Arias was ready to hear Usam's version of things. Although he had not had any chance of talking to his mom about his possible involvement with all three of her nieces, he knew somehow, very soon, something would happen from his end.

"Look, I know him very well. I just know when something is off, with him"

"I hear you. I've told him many times my feelings about things. But,..."

"Anyhow, I'll let him know you passed by, Arias. Trust me. He will get what's coming to him."

Arias wasn't sure how to analyze the conversation. But, he understood from Usam's stance on discipline, that eventually, Lars would conform to standards and norms.

In most cultures, it appears that brotherly love and affection can be painfully felt, if there is a clash in personality. Usam and Lars, brothers, who appeared clearly tied to an upper level of society, had to somehow overcome the potential devastation and descent to unacceptance and barring by some.

With intervention, or through an ideal manner of instruction, obtaining wisdom would perhaps be possible.

When Arias began to process what had just happened, he felt relieved that he was not feeling the pressure alone. He also began to understand that perhaps certain feelings had to be suppressed for his own sanity.

He finally reached home. Sitting in his car, he placed a phone call to Sino. She responded on the second ring. "Hello"

"Hi Sino, ...have a minute?"

"Yes, I do...tell me what's going on?"

"I went to his usual hangout. I met him"

"And...?"

"He seemed nice. ...Smelled good...looked good...and all that..."

"And"?

"I asked him, point blank...are you persecuting your ex wife?"

"What did he respond"?

"He chuckled a bit, and asked why I was asking him such a thing, if I was some kind of a private detective or investigator?"

"then, what did you say...?"

"I said, look..., someone dear to me, likes her, and I would hate to see something really awful happens here.., so let me ask you again, are you persecuting her?"

"and then he said "No", right?"

"Yes, he said "No", but he said he knew who was persecuting her, that it wasn't him"

"But, did you press on the topic, to try to get him to say something?"

"yes. Something was off, though. As we became friendly, ordering drinks, he said the most unusual thing"

"What's that?"

"He asked me if I ever ate the skull of a goat"

"What?"

"You did tell me that your bible member, sensed diabolical things happening to her, right?"

"Right"

"There you have it, this man is a diabolical %%#%%#..., you hear me."

"Then, what happened"?

"He didn't say anything else that was off. I wouldn't go near him again even if you paid me a million bucks...you hear"?

"Thanks Arias...I appreciate your help."

"Anytime, my dear cousin..., if you need anything else, please let me know..."

"Ok. I guess I can mention this to her, to see what can be done. But, thanks so much.

"Anytime...Bye for now"

Sino clicked her phone and just stood there. She wasn't sure how to comprehend it all. Then, her thoughts were traveling. "*she even fears falling asleep, with a phone next to her, as if fearing being used under an occult scheme? What kind of people have those kinds of power to actually touch someone's body, from another site...and...and...launch a hypnotic mechanism, or...in her case, a spirit, evil at that..., to do their deeds. This is criminal...Arias didn't question that man enough..., he said it wasn't him..?so he should have asked him who is involved in this thing, here...I simply don't know how to help her...this is hopeless...No, not hopeless...there's always Hope, for a better turnout...Anyway, I think I'll talk to the deacon. I know he'll say, "if the truth is on her side, the Lord will shield her from evil"..and that's true...The book of Deuteronomy admonishes the occult, and diabolical forces...*"

So, her thoughts were bent on comprehension. She began to realize that there was a great deal of evil in this world. The

ability to interfere in someone's quest for living is an abomi-
nation. Only Almighty God has the power to cease and desist
basic human capacity. Those who do so, are competing with
God. So, the premise of competition is by no means valid,
fully knowing the Almighty powers of God, his son, and the
Holy Spirit.

From this concept, life is a gift from God. Those, whose
knowledge emphasizes a desire to control people's lives, for
their own benefit, lack wisdom and understanding of biblical prophecy.

Mota was typing away on her Hp laptop, summarizing her
findings on a project she was engaged in overseeing. She took
a break every now and then, to drink hot chocolate, or Yogi
tea. Standing by her bay window, she focused on the view of
a mountain directly across from her rental. The scenery was
so breathtaking, that she began to visualize certain things.
She saw herself as a young girl, running in the park, and fan-
tasizing on reaching her highest potential; She saw herself
talking to Tam, her sister, about life in general, and what her
expectations for her own life were. Then, with the reminiscing
mentally real on her mind, she remembered to call Sti. She
wanted to be updated on anything she had to be updated on,
if at all possible.

When she called Sti, she felt somewhat relieved that Sti's
report on her husband
was positive. Sti revealed her feelings to her when she
observed that a young lady had been living there; and the
gardener confirmed that it was not anything suspicious;
and her subsequent visit to Roi, etc. etc. She also mentioned
that her most current observations seemed to indicate a
change. "How so?"

"Well, a couple of times, I drove around and noticed, the Bromar that I met a few days earlier, seemed different."

"In what way, is she different"?

"Her clothes, her makeup, her entire self, seemed unusual, when I compared her to the person that I actually had the privilege to meet."

So, the conversation went on for close to an hour; with Mota, needing more information to attempt to analyze the situation. Mota also explained that Martin had been a long time friend to Roi; and that Martin's new marriage was a devastating blow to Bromar, because she loved her mom so much. From Mota's assertions, Sti was totally relieved that her initial suspicions were uncalled for. While ending the conversation, Sti suggested that they hit the town for a night cap. Mota agreed to meet with her friend, later on that day.

Upon hanging up, and restarting her work where she left off, Sino walked past her and said, "Mom, I think Tori has a boyfriend"...

"Are you sure?"

"Yes, she was very cozy on the phone with someone the other day."

"Wow, I wonder why she didn't discuss anything with me about that..."

"Anyway, I just thought I'd say something."

"How is your bible study group project coming along?"

"It's coming along well. I am trying to help the lady I spoke to you about. Anyhow, she may get some assistance from the deacon."

"That's great to hear. It's amazing how some youngsters possess better cognitive abilities, than us, older folks...Anyway, don't get yourself too involved.But, it's nice that you're trying to make a difference in her life...Proud of you."

Chapter 6

"Thanks mom... I am going out for a few...I won't be too late."

"All right...just be careful."

A mother who constantly cares for her children tends to be anxious and nervous about their activities, whereabouts, etc. at all times. Although Mota cared very much for her daughters, she trusted them with her entire being. Not knowing at all times where they are was not a concern that she cared to explore emotionally.

After the completion of her work, she tidied up her workstation; and went about getting ready for her date with Sti, her good and trusting friend.

Around the same time, Tori was rushing back home, from a date with Lars. He presented himself as Eon, to Tori. The triple formation of his name apparently earned him the right to introduce himself in partial names. His first and middle names were actually Lars Eon Aron. They met at a museum, where Tori wanted to learn about artifacts from any historical events. After approaching her, fully knowing her name, her heart was melted right away. Their first date consisted of walking in park and his surroundings. Their second date was a movie event that was actually a drive-in. But, after she dropped him off, he inadvertently left an item in her car–a diamond studded ornament that was very valuable. The ornament was boxed and given to him by a friend who asked him to hold on to it.

The idea of retaining something of value without being made aware of what it was, where it came from, and why it was not safely guarded somewhere, can be a detriment, depending on the source of it, and the motive for having it.

Tori rushed back home, with the notion that she had found the right man for her. It was somewhat the premise of "Love at first sight" However, the twist remains that an implication of a crime has surfaced. Unknowingly, she left the ornament in her car, when she reached home.

Chapter 7

Entanglements of sorts
Derivation of wrong
Streaming from different ports
Just like a song

Roi woke up very early to go jogging. He placed his keys in his sweat pants' right pocket, and his apple watch in his left. As he began his jogging routine, he felt mesmerized by the sceneries, a pond on his left, and the highest mountain in the region on his right. Sadness was not a sentiment he embraced. He knew he missed his family. As a matter of fact, he kept in close contact with all three of his daughters. His last conversation with Mota, was peaceful. No accusations on the $35,000 bonus; no negativity. He felt grateful that somehow, they were getting along. Something didn't seem right with Biamu. He sensed a bit of hesitation, when he last conversed with her. He clearly remembered what she uttered, the last time he spoke to her. *"Why couldn't you get along with mom?"*

That last question lingered on his mind for a long time. His thoughts were interrupted by the sound of his cell phone, which he kept at the upper edge snapped on his T-shirt. He almost ignored it; but he picked up. "Hello"

"Are you Roi..?"

Before the caller stated his last name. He answered "Yes, I am. Who is this?"

"Sir, do you have a Range Rover registered in your name?"

"Yes, I do. And you are?"

"Oh, yes, I am sorry. I am a detective, attached to the XXC precinct. My name is Tim"

"Detective? What's going on"?

"Yes, there is a tracking device that has been linked to that particular car. Can you tell me anything about what I am talking about?

"I am perplexed. My daughter, Tori is driving the car. The Range Rover is registered in my name; but, I haven't seen it in a few months now. Can you tell me what this is about?"

"Are you in a position to visit us, say, in about two hours? I will gladly give you all the details that you need."

"Certainly, I can. "

"See you then."

Roi hung up; and wondered what this was about.

He made a mental note to call Tori, as soon as his jogging ended. He was not about to turn around right then, to fully grasp what was happening.

Meanwhile, Arias kept pacing back and forth, trying to understand why Lars wanted to mess up their friendship. He thought about telling his mom, but refrained from doing so, without knowing for sure what his plans were. A few minutes earlier, He and Lars agreed to meet at their usual hangout, after school.

Prior to meeting with him, he was attempting to formulate his own plan, to protect his cousins.

He knew for sure that what he had found out about a cult, tied to Lars, could not be real. First, he had to do some investigative work, for Sino; then, he began to feel the need to do the same with his friend.

Usam, on his end, had requested assistance from a close friend. The friend, attended a couple of meetings where Lars frequented and witnessed some unusual demands. One of which dealt with a "Dare" "*We dare you to do something strange within such and such a period. If you don't, you will be crowned as a defeated member...*"type of pressure. On one particular day, ZT, (Usam's friend) sat all the way at the back of a darkened room. Lars had been initiated at the previous session, which ZT had not attended. But, he was able to infer that Lars had been accepted as a member. The specifics of the initiation could not fully be assessed; but, he opined that it had been a gross process, from the high-fives, and other gestures.

His report about what he had witnessed was given both in writing, and verbally.

"I don't think this cult, is a boy club, if you know what I mean"he said during his conversation with Usam.

"I figured that..."

"What are you going to do?"

"I will do what I think he deserves"

"Do you want me to go back there?"

"I guess you may..., but you know, I think I have enough information to confirm what I suspected all along."

"What are you going to do to him?"

"Don't worry about it. I have a couple of things to do. Thank you for everything; and keep me posted, will you?"

"Of course...you got it, man"

After a conversation, involving his younger brother, Usam knew what to do right away. He placed a sticky note on Lars' bedroom door: "*I need to talk to you when you get home. It's urgent.*"

Roi reached home on time, to get ready for a meeting at the precinct. As he jumped in the shower, he made a mental note to call Tori.

With a myriad of issues, challenging as these may have been, Roi always kept himself above reproach. With a somewhat narcissistic personality, he prided himself on his ability to juggle things as they were presented. Never once, did he doubt that his wife would not return. He felt comfortable to take action whenever action needed to be taken. Part of his self confidence originated from his upbringing, where all of his achievements were recorded by his parents; even when he participated in spelling bees, finishing 7th place. He would often hear his father say: *"No achievement is too small to acknowledge."*Anything of great value to his parents, became of great value to him. He was nurtured to understand right from wrong; and on the downside, to "tell it like it is", no matter how hurtful. So, his personality was shaped to be the man that he became, making it hard for Mota, at times, struggling keeping the marriage going forward.

He got out of the shower; dressed and headed out, with his cell phone to his right ear, hearing the ring that was finally picked up. "Hi Dad"

"Tori, what's going on with the car?"

"What do you mean? the car is fine"

"I am on my way to see a detective, who called me to say a tracking device is in the car. "

"What? I don't know what he is referring to."

"Well, then, stay by your phone, I'll call you as soon as I know more"

"Oh, Great...what do you think this is about?"

"If I knew I would blurt it out. I was hoping you'd tell me..."

"I don't know...so, Ok, just let me know what you find out"

Chapter 7

"Will do...stay by your phone."

"I will."

Roi sat in his car; started the engine to roll backward out of the driveway. He glimpsed sideways, and saw Bromar pulling up. He waved; and backed out of the driveway.

He smiled as he remembered his good works to discipline that girl.

On the way over to the police station, his mind was on overdrive, imagining what was going on with Tori and Biamu. He knew for sure, the issue with the car had some sort of illegality that he was definitely not prepared to deal with.

He reached the station on time. He walked in and asked for Detective Tim. He was directed to have a seat, and wait. He looked at his watch, knowing how full his schedule for his work was. But, he prioritized his visit to the station, compared to others. His observations led him to believe that the facility was newly built. He had expected to see some outcasts of society, handcuffed, sitting with their lawyers, waiting to be heard. Quite the contrary, he was alone with his thoughts, pondering what the car situation was.

A few minutes passed by, when Detective Tim walked out to greet him. "Thank you for coming promptly, please follow me..."

Roi stood up, slightly before the detective shook his hand. He followed the detective to a small interrogation room. He told Roi where to sit, and motioned for him to wait. Roi sat down, wondering again the extent of what the issue was. Understanding vaguely how police work is very distinct, he knew not to talk about anything. The detective came back in with another detective, and introduced him as Detective Matt. He nodded, and simply waited.

"Mr. Roi, why don't you tell us why we're here." The younger officer Matt said.

"Am I being placed under arrest?"

"It depends, what do you think?"

"I'll have you know that I am an upstanding figure in this community, and when I am being charged for something, I know beforehand. I would come accompanied with my attorney, if I knew what this was about. Furthermore, my daughter doesn't understand what you are referring to either..."

Tim stood up, and walked around Roi to face him. He raised his right arm and tapped at a picture on the wall, with loud bangs, as if trying to make a point.

Roi still could not understand what was being said.

"Excuse us for a moment."

Both officers walked out and were observing Roi from a double sided glass, that rendered them invisible from their side.

"You see, Matt, this experience will teach you something valuable. I tapped on the picture on the wall, to trigger a reaction. Do you see a reaction from him?"

"Nothing at all. I think we should go back in and get the truth out of him"

"No. We're done. He didn't even glance at the picture twice. I noticed that he looked at it, then dismissed any thoughts...No, he is telling the truth. He doesn't know anything about this..."

"So, what do we do now? We know where the ornament is. Do we go and fetch it?"

"No. Again. We have to know who stole it from the museum. It isn't him. Just follow my lead."

After a few minutes, they both walked back in.

"You're free to go. I will be in touch with your daughter"

"Detective Tim, I need to know what this is about. You mentioned there was a tracking device in the car?"

"I will grant you the courtesy of a full explanation, after I speak to your daughter"

"I don't like this. Does she need a lawyer?"

"It depends. Thank you. We'll be in touch"

Roi walked out with a perplexed look on his face, wondering what, how, where, and when?

A large picture of the diamond studded ornament was on the wall, to trigger some type of reaction from whomever. The detective in charge of the investigation, considered one of the best in his station, knew exactly how to resolve the case. What Lars' connection didn't know was that those types of pricey items were secured with a tracking device attached on the surface of the items.

Usam, on his end, was looking forward to interrogating Lars. He became slightly impatient, pacing back and forth. His parents noticed the friction between the two brothers, but didn't get involved, except to ask, the night before "Anything wrong between you two?", to which Usam answered: "Not 100% sure yet, but nothing I can't resolve." His parents were very busy people, involved in the foster care field. Busy, and caring people.

Usam decided to walk into Lars' room, and started searching for anything which could spark his explanations for getting involved. He searched through each drawer of the dresser, chest, and the nightstands. Nothing stood out. He searched more carefully in one of the nightstands, and noticed a worn-out book with lots of pages that were not bound. He flipped through it, and found some post it notes that were not totally understood. But, he decided it was a great way to know a bit more about his brother. He took it; closed the door behind him, left the note he had placed earlier on the door; and went to his own room.

He began to read from page 1. When he reached about the middle of the book, something startled him a bit. In diary form,

Lars wrote in the book that one day, he will visit "Dracula's mansion in Mongolia; He also, one day, wants to learn about the Apatani Tribeswomen in Africa; and wants to make research on Ella Harper, the camel girl" Usam continued reading and bingo – he found the "Dare" In the diary, it reads: "*..I met all 3. All 3 will fall head over heels in love..., then I'll gladly tell them the truth, after I win my "Dare"award, then, the boys will respect me as their own. Poor little girls, so pretty, so naïve, Oh, there's nothing I can do to stop what I want to do, but, it will happen...*"

The rest of his written comments could not be any worse than what was already written. Usam slammed the book shot, and felt enraged. Then, he began to think: "*...Ok, little brother, that's the kind of work you're doing out there.., I will teach you a lesson...*"Usam took the book back to Lars' room then slammed the door behind him.

Several blocks away, Mota received a phone call from Roi, explaining the developments of what had just surfaced. With questions that remained unanswered, Mota was extremely confused. Roi's tone of voice was calm, and assumed unalarming from Mota's viewpoint. He assured her that he would be there for Tori, at the station.

The detective was able to reach Tori, and set up an appointment for later in the day.

Mota sat there at her desk; with millions of thoughts roaming in her head. The night before, she had a date with Sti. She remembered how she described a weird dream she experienced a couple of nights prior. She saw herself being stranded on a deserted road..."*where she apparently had run out of gas. Sitting there, waiting for a car to pass by, was very terrifying. She waited and waited. No one came to help her. Then, she started up the engine again, and saw silhouettes from the clouds coming toward her. Startled by the sight, she woke up...*"

Chapter 7

When she described the dream to Sti, she felt reassured that it was simply a dream; not anything to have been alarmed about; as Sti remained silent. Usually, Sti would have a biblical explanation right away. The explanation of the dream ended with one question from Sti: "...*Did you recognize any faces of the silhouettes?* to which Mota responded "No."

Thinking about the time she spent, having a good time, unbeknownst to her that her daughter had been involved in an infraction of some sort, tore at her being in full force.

She promised that she would also be at the station.

Several blocks away, at school, during breaks, Arias and Lars engaged in chitchatting, about their most recent quests. With a project completed, Arias felt more than pleased about helping Sino figure certain things out. Although he would have concurred to continue probing into Sino's friend's life, he chose to bow out of such, for his lack of comfort mentally, particularly due to the involvement of the occult. As he felt interested in knowing more about Lars' activities, he confirmed with displeasure, that Lars was indeed dating all three of his cousins. "Do you realize what I am feeling right now, knowing what I know? Do you?"

"Just relax, man, nothing is happening. But, I think Tori is totally in love with me"

"I don't think you fully feel me, Lars Aron, you are playing with my life, doing what you're doing. I am not approving this... no, no...you're not truly my friend..."

Back and forth, a disagreement ensued. Arias felt betrayed, and slightly angry. Lars, on the other hand, wasn't too sympathetic about everything. They ended the disagreement. As they parted, Lars blurted out: "Just relax, nothing is happening..."

Arias walked to his car, and headed home.

Further away from that site, Tori was sitting in an interrogation room, by herself, as two Officers from an observation point, were recording her demeanor, and her moves. Although she had reported as scheduled, the leading detective was not there yet. She arrived at relatively the same time as Roi, as she was just as curious to deal with the issue as he was. Mota also reported there slightly later than they appeared. Both Roi and Mota, were sitting on a bench, outside in the lobby area, anxious, and nervous about what the issue was.

After close to an hour, the lead detective walked in, offering Tori a bottle of water. He came in with a rookie detective, introducing him, as a supporting detective. They both sat down. Tori took the bottle and set it on the table. "You don't know why you're here, Do you"?

"There's a tracking device in my car? why?"

Attempting to fully grasp what the inference was, Tori kept quiet, and listened to Detective Tim's words; although she still could not understand.

"Ms. May I have your car keys, for a few minutes"?"

"Why?"

"I need to make you understand what it is that we're trying to find out"

"Yes, of course"

She stood up, and fetched her keys from her jeans' pockets. She was still not in the least mindful of the ornament that she was asked to retain.

The detective took the keys, and said "Excuse us for a minute"

Tori was again observed. The same assessment was made, that she was not aware of anything. "She isn't even looking at the picture on the wall"

"You're right" The rookie detective agreed.

Chapter 7

The ornament was still in the car, as the detectives, both walked over to the parking lot, open the car door in the back-seat, and retrieved the box.

Meanwhile, Roi observed what was happening, and inferred that perhaps Tori needed a lawyer. He got on his phone to reach his attorney, and explained what he felt was happening. Mota, on the other hand, simply shook things off, and became calm, as if she knew for a fact, that her daughter would be cleared of whatever it was, that was occurring.

Detective Tim walked in with the box, and set it on the table; then gave her back her keys. He then, said "Excuse us for a minute."

They both walked out and observed her again.

This time, they observed that she looked at the box, and seemed to somewhat remember something.

"Do you see anything criminal about her demeanor?"

"Not really. She seems to be remembering something. She looks a little nervous."

"...But, not criminal?"

"Precisely"

Detective Tim was further assessing the situation, while also training his rookie partner. "Now, I think I understand what happened here...Ok, let's go back in."

They entered the room.

"Where did you get this box from?"

"A friend of mine told me to keep it for him"

"Why did you keep the knowledge of this from us?"

"I don't know what you mean"

"I know you don't. But, you need to cooperate with us and tell us everything we need to know"

"Of course"

"Who gave this to you? his name, address, phone number... everything you know about this person."

Tori went on to provide "Eon"'s name, address, and phone number. She even offered to call him right then and there. They allowed her to. When there was no answer, she left a message. "Hi Eon, I am at the police station, because of a tracking device on the box, that I kept in my car. Please call me back ASAP...Thanks."

At such a juncture, at least the police station had finally come to an impasse, having a direct lead to either convict, and punish. At least, that was their opinion. Detective Tim also placed a call to Eon, asking him to pass by the station. Although he had the option of picking him up, since his address was known, he wanted to give him the liberty of coming in on his own. Of course, if he had not responded, a cruiser would have had no choice but to report to his home, with a warrant.

Such was hardly necessary.

Lars did show up after receiving the message from both Tori, and Detective Tim. He was placed under the same routine, as Roi and Tori, with same observations. Except this time, the box was placed on the table. Without even looking at the picture on the wall, Lars immediately recognized the box. They observed his demeanor, looking at the box, and thinking of something which could not yet be determined. Detective Tim noticed that he glimpsed at the picture, but did not seem to connect the two items, the box and the picture. After what seemed to be 30 minutes, both officers walked in and sat down.

"What are we doing here, Eon? Can you help us out here?"

"My girlfriend tells me there was a tracking device in her car. But, I am assuming this box, which I was holding for a friend of mine, was part of the tracking device component of this...?"

"Tell us more."Detective Tim asked, as the rookie detective looked on, with diminished, and accusatory eyes.

"A friend told me to hang on to this for him…"

"Why did you give it to your girlfriend to hold?"

"I didn't mean to. One day, she dropped me off at home; and I simply forgot to take it with me."

"Who asked you to hold on to it…?"

So, the interrogation went on for another 45 minutes. Name, address, and phone number of the friend was provided.

Detective Tim didn't assess any reasons why to hold Lars in custody. But, he advised him not to go out of state, until his information on the friend checked out. Lars agreed; and said: "Of course…"

The investigatory routine went on. The friend was deemed innocent, based on the same demeanor exhibited as Lars's. But, the friend of the friend, was the last to be interrogated. As soon as they began to observe his demeanor, they *knew he was the culprit. He saw the picture on the wall and freaked out,* actually imagining a way out. Detective Tim, while observing, called for backup, to place him under arrest. A total number of eight officers were summoned, just in case he was armed with anything.

On the day Lars was interrogated, he was somewhat traumatized, wondering what had transpired exactly, with the box a friend had asked him to hold on to. He was more traumatized when Usam handed him a pamphlet, with a series of scriptural verses, upon telling him he was grounded, or else.

He entered his room and figured out everything. His drawers were ransacked, and a couple of other things hanging out of his nightstands caught his attention. He immediately surmised that Usam had read his diary. He thought to himself:

"*Oh, Great…I am done.*"

As a person in his late teens, he always looked up to his brother, with respect. He also appreciated his support when he needed it; keeping their parents out of the loop; particularly when Usam could resolve an issue.

Lars looked at the pamphlet; skimmed through it, and realized that Usam had put it together specifically for this occasion. He began reading it: .1Corinthians 14:33..."For God is not a God of confusion but of peace..."... Romans 16:18 such persons do not serve the Lord, but their own appetites, and by smooth talk and flattery deceive the hearts of the naïve".. Psalm 119:169..."Let my cry come before you, Oh, Lord! Give me understanding according to your word"..Psalm 119:34 "Give me understanding that I may keep your law and observe it with my whole heart..."..2Timothy 1:7..."For God gave us a spirit not of fear, but of power, and love and self control..."

As Lars continued to read the scriptures, he saw a note from Usam: "If you're thinking about Jeremiah 17:9 "The heart is deceitful above all things, and desperately sick, who can understand it?", Then this is my resolution for your condition – Psalm 101.7 "No one who practices deceit shall dwell in my house..."

Please make yourself available today"

Lars took the pamphlet, set it aside, and lay down on his back on his bed, feeling slightly trapped.

Certain people, at times, need self discipline in order to navigate through life without hurting others. The maneuvering, whether it be taught, realized on own recognizance, or from any other means, can be pleasing, having the correct mindset to reach goals. In Lars' case, there may have been one primary objective, that triggered a need to prove his manhood, or his popularity. Such was geared toward recognition, and boosting of his ego. As fortunate as it sounds, having a relative who cares enough to take a stand, the drawback that exists relates to a possible withdrawal from inner realization. In other words, it would be fair to assess that, feelings of inadequacy and thoughtlessness would result in his psyche, proceeding forward.

Chapter 8

Sign of the times
Linking innocence to the unknown
Presented as rhymes
As in devotion with a crown

Roi was standing by his window, at home, replaying on his mind what transpired a couple of days prior. On a cold morning, where, the air looked stifling, without proper winter gears, and the windshields on the cars were filled with what seemed like icicles, no one would imagine what was twirling in Roi's head. He imagined being on vacation in Maui, with his entire family by his side. On his vacation, he saw himself on a beach with Mota, keeping quiet about the mess, she had made, moving out of their home. He also surmised he would be smiling secretly for having had the understanding to allow his entire family to go on its way, to wherever to find itself. Chuckling a little, he simply could not believe what he had been through with Tori's explanations for the reason why there was an expensive stolen item in her car. He also could not understand Mota's reassurance that everything was A-OK. As he stood there, he remembered the exact moment he realized he had had enough.

On that day, Tori drove behind her parents who headed straight to their regular home. As they pulled up on the driveway, Mota felt a sense of sadness, because of the day on which she made her decision to leave. They got in, right before Tori stepped out, left the door ajar for her. Mota looked around and saw that nothing had changed. The house looked exactly the way she had left it. Tori stepped in and simply sat down on the sofa, and fetched her phone to again leave a message for Eon.

She texted him: "I left you a voicemail regarding the box. Apparently the box had a tracking device...I just left the police station. What is going on? Please text me back. I am worried."

Eon responded: "I am getting ready now to go to the police station. A Detective Tim, left a message, as well. I sincerely dk what's up either. I'll keep you posted."

As Tori was about to text again, Roi came and sat right across from her. She put the phone away, and stared into space. "Ok, young lady,...care to tell me what's going on? Do you think you need a lawyer?"

"No. I don't think that. The police is getting in touch with Eon. He's the one who gave me the box to hold"

"Who is Eon? Hey Mota, who is Eon?"

Mota walked nonchalantly across the room, and said: "Gee, Roi, why don't you ask Tori who he is? I don't know...I have never heard that name before..."

Tori felt ashamed, and said: "He is a friend.., I met him a few weeks ago..."

"...And...he gave you a package to keep? and you didn't question it..?"

"I thought I'd give it back on the same day he told me to hold on to it, but, I just forgot to give it to him when I dropped him off..."

Roi stood up, and tried to control his temper in the best approach possible. Every time, he felt the urge to blame Mota for not even knowing who this man was, he suppressed his feelings more and more.

So the day continued with questioning along the lines of who Eon's family was, where he lived, went to school, his activities, etc. to which Tori revealed what she knew and nothing more.

Roi remembered the day as clear as crystal and smiled slightly because he had received a letter from Detective Tim, explaining everything.

He dialed Mota's number while standing by the window, and left a message: "I received a letter from Detective Tim. Apparently, this whole mess was a problem in the form of a "Package being held for a friend of a friend of a friend" The culprit was apprehended. He took a museum ornament...Anyway, call me back when you get this...Thank you"

Roi felt relieved, thinking again about being on vacation. His thoughts were interrupted by the sound of the doorbell. He opened up the door, and moved aside for Martin who had loads of groceries to carry in. Roi and Martin had been such close friends for a long time, and trusted each other very very much. He walked in with the groceries, set them on the island piece in the kitchen and said: "Thank you, Pal..."As he attempted to catch his breath. Never once, had Roi asked him when he would allow his daughter to come live with him. Martin was grateful for the turnaround in Bromar's life and wondered how Roi managed such a transition. Although he never asked him how he did it, he smiled to himself at times, and thought Roi's place was the best venue for Bromar's direction for the time being. They sat as always in a small break room, where

Roi set up office space for himself. "So, are you giving back the $35K?"Martin asked.

"I thought about it for a long time..., but, not sure yet..."

"Aside from this questionable bonus, anything else wrong?"

Martin noticed the change in his demeanor, and pondered what the matter was.

In response to Martin's questions, he simply stated: "All's well that ends well"

"I guess you don't want to talk about it. I get it...No sweat, pal, You know I am here. By the way, when is Mota coming home?...My God, it's been close to a year."

"Soon, I think..."

With that, Roi jumped into another conversation to sway away from having to discuss Tori's recent case. Martin was his best friend. He knew that by the day after, he would be ready to talk about everything with him. He was worried about the "Eon person", to actually make a full assessment of what he was dealing with. He planned to look him up in social media, to fully grasp the kind of person his daughter was friending.

Meanwhile, Tam was sitting right across from Mota, pondering how to gently break the news of what she knew. On the day, her son, Arias walked in telling her to sit down before he could divulge such an atrocity, she had been rejoicing over finishing her manuscript, for book #8.

Having known the level of parenting dedicated to Mota's children, by their parents, made it extremely difficult to formulate on her mind how she was going to make the big reveal.

Tam and Mota had been close knit prior to Mota's marriage to Roi. Tam could never achieve any type of synchronization with Roi's personality. She respected him, from a father figure viewpoint, and his ways of disciplining. However, his off the wall comments would most times, strike an awful chord in

Tam's psyche. He would often ask her condescendingly when she would become a best selling storyteller. "I enjoy reading your tales, but, really..?"This question would linger on Tam's mind for a long time. Fortunately, Tam had never given up on her writing. She gained respect from certain circles; and believed she would one day become an inspiration.

Mota sat right across from her, on the phone, with Sti. "Yes, apparently, it was a package for a friend of a friend, on behalf of another friend saga...But, the important thing is, I think Tori has learned something from this..."

While Mota talked on the phone, Tam was rehearsing on her mind how she was going to reveal what she knew. The mental rehearsal began; but was interrupted, as she heard Mota releasing Sti from the conversation. "...My sister is here. So, I'll catch up with you, later...Ok. Bye..."

She stopped for a minute, to jot a note on a pad, while saying..."Tam, you would not believe what we just went through. But, that can wait...on the phone, you sounded very concerned about something..."

Tam smiled. She looked at the floor to gain her mental composure. Mota knew her sister very well, and immediately knew there was a pressing issue that was urgent. "Why do you look like that? Something is terribly wrong, right? Is it Arias? Or Mat? What is it, Tam?"

"It's not as bad as I am thinking right now, but, Arias came to me the other day to tell me something..."

"What is it about?"

"He tells me he has a friend, who is part of a cult, that is not exactly what you would call a boys scout club..."

"Yeah.., Go on Tam, you're scaring me"

"Oh, I am sorry. He caught me off guard, when he came home that day. He seemed extremely upset. He said to me that his friend Lars Aron is interested in all three of the girls."

"What girls?My girls?"

"I don't know much more than this. He didn't confirm to me if in fact he was dating them."

"Dating them? A cult member...dating my daughters?"

"I am sorry, Mota, I don't know how else to say this. I guess you should confer with them to get the story. Do they agree? Or don't they know that about this man?

Tam felt a headache coming on as she blurted out those words. Mota, on the other hand, sat down with her hand on the right side of her head, trying to remember the name Tori mentioned. "I know that Tori is friending someone named Eon."

"The best thing to do is to speak to all three at the same time.

An advice from a concerned sister is invaluable. From the gravity of her revelation, several inferences come to mind. How involved are these girls with Lars? And how damaged psychologically will they be when all is said and done?

These questions were roaming on Mota's mind; and actually kept her frozen for a few minutes. With a personality that offers endurance at all times, her absorption of this new knowledge took effect fairly quickly.

Meanwhile, life for several people involved, became threatening with respect to the foregoing. Usam sat at the table with his parents, waiting for some sort of reaction after he informed them of what he would do should his ultimatum not work. His father kept quiet, enjoying his soup; while his mother followed suit. Not to alarm either one, He did the same. Although rarely, did he eat dinner at the table, he felt compelled to enjoy the moment, not to boast, but to somehow connect to his parents on a higher level. He was not shocked when his mother blurted out – "Well, you see, something like that would never happen to any of us; our bloodline is too strong and divine. We adopted Lars when he was eight months old..."In response, Usam simply said: "I overheard that conversation when I was ten. But, I loved him, and still love him as if he were my own brother."

The table became even more quiet. His mother could not believe he knew all along.

Usam kept certain things to himself. He did not divulge that one of Lars' friends, took a museum ornament on a "Dare", from the same cult; And that the police was investigating the entire club, to recommend its closure.

On a mission to save his brother's life, Usam dropped everything, and demanded that he resume a life on the right path.

Around the same time, Roi was slightly taken aback by his normal work routine, and decided to phone a private investigator, who had been a friend at one point in his life. He was uncertain as to what he would find out, but his instincts drove him to believe such was the right approach to take.

His routine involved working on several personnel issues at the office, with flexibility to work from home. One of his cases dealt with realigning personnel, others dealt with budgeting for specific departmental functions, and certain cases called for his judgment in determining hiring and firing.

A particular colleague who had had a pressing matter plaguing his entire life was very pleased with this P.I.'s involvement.

One of the things Roi needed to find out involved Lars' family, his academic record, and his activities. Most importantly, he needed to have complete secrecy about his quest to know and be in the know.

The type of psychology that can be described in such a situation relates to a desire to control, and plan. Planning in such an instance would be geared toward a strategy to stop and discontinue certain ties; or approaching an outcome with an open mind. From Roi's viewpoint, he would have rather get close to Lars to learn everything about him, and proceed with a reversed type of psychology, to end the ties that bound him to his daughter. A father, in a situation where, a potential suitor, for his daughter, is found involved (through friendship with others), in criminal activities, can understandably react adversely to such a courtship. Roi's personality prevented him from being openly upset.

At the moment where he left a voicemail message for the P.I., he received a phone call from a colleague, requesting his presence at a conference, the following week. He stated that he would be there.

A couple of days later, he was seated at a conference table, listening to his colleagues discuss an Occult case, involving a former employee. As they kept going back and forth, that such and such was the real issue, Roi surmised that in an occult case, only one side benefitted. Whoever was receiving full benefits of the case, was the one to investigate and reprimand. The whole discussion centered around years and years of apparent abuse of a person, whose surveillance never really disclosed any criminal activities. However, during the wee hours of the night, a certain group surfaced around her area to do what? No one knew. Roi kept asking, Has she complained to anyone in the company? When was the last time she worked here? What was the reason for her separation? Why do we keep tabs on her whereabouts? And why has she not been called to a hearing where all disclosures could be made?

Roi was not happy with the answers, which were vague, and lacked any real meanings. The discussions continued for at least four hours. At the end of the conference, there was no conclusion.

He felt disappointed, thinking about the case as he drove home. He pulled up on his driveway, and sat there for a few minutes. When his thought process relaxed a bit, he came out of the car, and walked to his front door. When he opened the door, he heard a conversation streaming from the kitchen. Because of his belief that parents ought to know everything that goes on in their children's lives, he stopped at the corner of the kitchen to listen. Although Bromar was not his own child, he treated her as if she had been. ".Yeah, he is crazy. I can't wait to turn eighteen, and get out of here...What? Oh, No, I don't want to go back there. My stepmother is a freak...I can't stand her Oh, I know...I can't do that...with everything I went through with his so called discipline, if I do this, he will freak me out... Never, he is not my father...and I prefer to keep thinking that it will be time to be on my own, next year...I can't believe I went through this, and I will definitely stay on his good side.., but, anyway, the day will come...what? yeah, I guess so...it definitely could be worse...he was kind enough to keep me here...yeah, he is a friend of my father's...Oh, no, he is not like that...he is just a little crazy when there's disrespect and all...Absolutely... Ok. call me later...Bye..."

Roi had a smirk on his face, and gently and quietly walked up the stairs. As he was happy with himself being successful at disciplining Bromar, he kept wondering which tactic worked the best. *"..I wonder if it was the dirt on the car...every time she washed it, and was ready to go wherever she wanted to be, the dirt got right back on (LoL)...; or maybe it was that actor who followed her everywhere, with a stick.; or was it the principal of the school (a good buddy of mine) who alerted her to the fact that she would be reprimanded on a lifetime duty of janitorial services, until she turned forty five...; or maybe the allowance thing..., reversal..., she would be paying me instead of my paying her...(LoL).*

These thoughts were amusing to Roi. From his perspective, disciplining no matter how done, was an absolute necessity. His amusing thoughts ceased when he came back to reality. A meeting with his P.I. was set for later in the week. Thinking about such a meeting created tension, since he was uncertain what dark aspect was there to be found out.

A couple of days earlier, Eon and Tori were seated at a drive-in. He had a great deal on his mind. Usam's ultimatum of 48 hours, stretched to 72 hours created so much pressure that at times he was not sure how to deal with his predicament. Tori noticed the change, and mentioned it. "...It's nothing, I just have a lot on my mind..."His explanation was brief, and seemed calculated. At the same time, he was planning on different approaches to break up with Tori. Two hours prior, He met with Biamu and told her point blank, it would not work, but, he still felt romantic feelings toward her. He fibbed by professing his love, and requested some time to think things over. The sad part is Biamu and Aron's meetings at his friend's place were more engaged than his dates with Tori and Sino. Biamu felt hurt, but agreed to keep in touch from afar, and promised that she would wait for him to make a decision.

Skillfully, he felt the praise from his club buddies, looking up to him, for managing such an intense situation. Although he had not admitted to his club, about planning to end the relationships, he had already made the decision to quietly bow out of the club. Not doing so, would harm his bond with his brother, Usam.

Toward the end of the night with Tori, Eon repeated the same approach, that he had practiced on Biamu. "I just need some time to think things over...; this is our last date as it stands now.., but as soon as I make a decision, I will let you know..."

"I don't understand. What do you mean? Ok, I get it, you were involved in the theft of that piece, weren't you? My God, I can't believe what you're telling me, right now. Ok. So, when will you make your decision?"

"I am sorry. Like I said, I'll let you know."

Back and forth, with tears in her eyes, Tori felt hurt, wanting to know why, if it was because of another girl, or because of her..., back and forth as they reached Eon's home. He got out, and said "So long."sadly.

Tori drove off, with a million questions.

The common theme displayed here, conveys sentiments of fleeing from danger. Bromar, on the one hand, did not sway from her newfound way of living, not only to discourage any reaction from Roi; but, also to be at peace with her rebellious ways. Similarly, Tori, after dropping off Eon, had many questions; but preferred to simply accept his explanations and not pursue any chance of a revival of the heart.

On the same night, Sino was completely stood up, by Lars. No explanation, nor even a phone call.

Chapter 9

A break-up, resulting
An ultimatum, honored
A note, procuring
Test of the heart, cornered

Sino was at her church, preparing for her class.
With her members, arriving one by one, she knew she
would have a full house. Her papers were in order, on top of
her homework from school. Her goals included a desire for
extreme exposure in Theology. Although she had not decided
on her direction fully, her psyche was wrapped around the
Word of God.

She greeted the members as they came in. She walked over
to her friend whose marriage had dissolved and was in need
of a helping hand. "Hi, so glad to see you again."

"Glad to be here, I do understand wat you said about talking
to the Deacon..."

"Yes, he agrees to pray with you, over this type of problem."

"I realize that I may never be able to resolve..."

"No, no, no, don't ever say "never"..., I've heard awful stories
that eventually had a pleasant ending. Don't be discouraged."

"It's always good to talk to you, Sino, I can't tell you how much I appreciate what you've done. I know he said, he 's not the one persecuting me, but, I also know the Lord has already witnessed all that he has done..."

"That's right. Ok, Have a seat, and we will be discussing some points in the bible..."

"Thank you. I will..."

Sino roamed around, and chatted with a few other members briefly, and began her meeting.

She took her notes and began to speak. After a few minutes, she continued..."..I was reading through biblical scripture and noticed a few things. One of which is the number of times, some words appear as the last word in the books of the bible. For instance, The divine name, Jesus, is the last word in the book of 1st Corinthians, and appears only once, as the last word. No other books display the name of the Lord as the last word. So are the words, "Lord", and "him"..., the last words in the book of Psalms, and the book of Acts, respectively. No other books display these words as the last word. Does anyone have any idea why that is? I also noticed, The divine words "God"and "Amen", appear in the books of "Luke, 2John, Amos, Nehemiah"; and "Romans, Galatians, 2Peter, and Jude", respectively, as the last words of these books. No other books display these words as the last word. Sometimes, when we read scripture, we have to understand our own interpretations. We can try to link the meaning of the divine name of Jesus, appearing only once, as the last word, in one book, as signifying his humility, and his simplicity in thoughts and in action; because the Father created him to be a savior of others. Does anyone have any input about these points?"

A lady, from the back, stood up, to make a point: "I agree that the Lord is so humble; that he wasn't meant to represent a focus point. If every last word in every book of the bible was his name, I think there would be a general implication that he wanted to be the main character in the Holy book; No, No,. I agree with you, there...Thank you."

Sino's meeting took close to two hours. Different interpretations were amazing in terms of he learning process of the Word.

At the end of the meeting, Sino prepared to leave and she began to think about the weirdness in her family. Lars, after standing her up the night before, did not call her to provide any explanations. She reached home early, the night before, as a result, and was met with concerns from her mom, who informed her that there was to be a family meeting the next day. She also remembered seeing Tori, and Biamu home, quite early, as well. At that point, she had not surmised what the specifics of an issue had been. She was ready for the family meeting, and left the church promptly.

Mota, right after her sister's visit, did not follow the advice given. Her sister left, a couple of hours after her revelations were made, and hugged her, while feeling really sorry. "Don't worry about us, we'll be fine."

"I will call you, tomorrow, to see how everything turned out."

"Thank you for telling me about this"was the last comment Mota had made to her sister.

But, of course, with different thoughts roaming through her mind, she wanted to call all of the girls right there, to tell them to get home, right away. But, she didn't. Her instincts navigated through her and made her feel hesitant to blurt out such a reveal. Close to two hours passed. She maintained her composure, thinking and trying to complete her work, when her phone rang. "Roi, what's going on?"

"You need to schedule a family meeting. We have an urgency..."

"What do you mean, urgency?"

I received a report from a P.I. that I hired. Tori needs to hear this, as well as Biamu and Sino..."

"Ok, I'll schedule it...what time?"

So, the meeting was scheduled for the day after.

On the one hand, it seems essential that parents, whose concerns for their children force them to take a firm stand to find answers, do take a stand; on the other, an action that involves a possible of invasion of privacy may in fact backfire and trigger a domino effect of issues. What of it, though, if in fact, searching for the nitty gritty allows for peace of mind.

Unknowingly, Lars, around the same time, was sitting down at his desk, at home, drafting a memo for Sino. He was unrecognizable, sitting at the meeting, and heard her questions during her meeting earlier. He wanted to explain and try to answer the biblical questions she brought up. Although he agreed somewhat with her assertions, he felt compelled to provide his own interpretations. His thoughts were geared toward not ever ask her to be involved with him, but to simply drop off his memo, at the church.

He edited his memo, typed it and printed it.

For assurance that it read correctly, he skimmed through it:

> *"..I've decided to write this memo to first of all thank you for a short friendship. By the time you read it, you will have known everything about me and my endeavors. But, please know that what transpired was not meant to hurt you. When I sat in your conference, the other day, I listened carefully to you and your teachings. Your insights into biblical scripture will take you far. But, I must complement what you said with this:*

Chapter 9

Jesus is Lord of Lords, King of Kings, the alpha, and Omega, the beginning and the end. Even though his name appears as the last word in one book of the "New Living Translation"version, please know that he is the beginning and the end of every book in the bible. Those of us who are used in his journey, are grateful to hold what we believe. While I take complete responsibility for my actions, I truly believe what I believe. What I believe will be known by you, one day. I cannot apologize to you, because of true insights on your part. Peace! LEA."...

Being satisfied with the memo, he stuffed it in an envelope.

Sino reached home at a relatively decent time. When she walked in, the mood was clear. The living room was quiet. Her father, mother and her sisters were waiting to begin. She said Hello; rushed into her room to drop off her handbag and papers, and came right back out.

Roi began by handing them copies of a report. He advised them to take their time to read it, and then ask questions.

The mood was that of a mixed reaction type thing. Biamu took it and sped out of the room, seemingly upset. Tori began by asking: "What is this Dad?""Why do you have to investigate everything about us?""We don't even live with you, anymore"... Obviously upset, Tori was rambling..."Lars Eon Aron."So, the report detailed what time he reached school, and outings with each one of them. The investigator even took pictures, when he was sitting next to Biamu, and in their cars. ..."*So, he called himself Eon, when he was with me; Lars, with Sino, and Aron with Biamu? why, how...How could I have been so stupid?"*Tori's thought process was devastatingly hurtful to her. "*...So, he* *thought he was Moses?I don't recall Moses dating all the sisters... Ok, I should have known...all the excuses when he could not be with me...Wow!.."*

Both Roi and Mota sat in silence. Mota looked at Tori and wanted to cry. Sino seemed in control. She kept quiet, and kept reading. Roi murmured to Mota that he needed to take Biamu for a psychological assessment, because he was worried.

Life lessons can be very difficult. From Lars' memo to Sino, it sounded clear that he felt he represented an aspect of their lives; as if prophetically. The question is: As much as he appeared to treasure his theological knowledge, would a higher power approve of his actions with these girls? Most likely not. Would the Lord agree with his deeds? Absolutely Not. From his standpoint, however, he felt no harm was intended and inflicted.

His brother Usam, knew of his deeds to neutralize the situation and felt compelled to ensure that his preachings were received in a manner conducive to normal standards.

Certain sayings about what's meant for harm, can be turned around for Good, may have been at play in these developments. A family in turmoil, surrounded by dark forces, triggering the need for them to separate, can at times unite in closeness in order to heal. What facilitates this type of closeness, depends on the will of the family members. A devastation can either fortify or diminish. In the case of Mota and Roi, the possibilities for a revival existed; as well as a turnaround that may deepen the wounds.

Biamu lay down on her bed, thinking about what could have been. She fantasized for a long time about becoming Aron's wife, and how many children they would have. She was grateful that she had not lost her innocence; although she came close to losing herself in the heat of passion.

Chapter 9

Tori stayed in her room, after letting her dad know that she did not appreciate what he had done. She did let him know, however, that she loved him, but simply could not tolerate his personality sometimes. To which, Roi responded: "I love you, too"; with a wink.

Sino simply kissed both her mom, and Dad on the cheeks, and said "Good night."

The differences in the manner in which these girls reacted may stem from individual personality traits, rather than common beliefs within the family structure.

While not much was said from Biamu, it appeared fully understood that her psyche had been much more traumatized in a way. But, the lessons would have had deeper consequences, had Usam not stepped in to expedite actions. By the same viewpoint, Arias had also intervened for the sake of his cousins.

Chapter 10

Moments of pondering
Leading to everlasting light
An ideal, a formation, thundering
Moulding the bonds from plight

The trees' leaves were garnering for a potential cleanup; yet, the scenery was breathtaking. Mota was on her regular walk; thinking about the developments in her life, in the two months prior. First, she kept wondering if she had done the right thing, delaying her return home. Secondly, she pondered on whether or not her initial reaction to leaving was rational and reasonable. To the latter, she surmised that she had made the right decision, since she learned a great deal more about her husband.

Just like Mota, Sino was in deep thoughts, wondering how she may have handled her situation better. She relived the day when she found a memo addressed to her, from Lars. At the beginning of that day, she drove up on the parking lot of the church and heard a commotion on the adjacent part of the lot. She felt curious and stopped to see what was happening. A small crowd circled a man, who appeared to be preaching; but, in fact he was just loudly expressing his views about "Injustice"

"*...If you're on the wrong side of the law, you cannot expect that concept to cover you...If you follow directions of law enforcement, it definitely applies to you...If you're demolishing properties to make a point, you can't expect support from that...If you speak up angrily, with a loud speaker, you better be sure that this concept covers you...if you're sleeping in your bed, and don't expect any visitors, and these visitors mistakenly shoot you, you better be sure this concept covers you...If you're on the right side, you don't trespass on people's properties, you don't persecute people, you don't gossip to gain favors against others; you don't force your barbaric religion on unwilling victims, you better be sure this concept covers you, and ...*"

Sino had heard enough, and with a smile, walked away, to go into the church. She surmised that the INJUSTICE movement, from this person's understanding was created to prevent people from being targeted only by virtue of their pigmentation. Her thoughts on this issue were passive as she fully understood the plight of Blacks, encountering and fighting discrimination.

On her regular desk, she found an envelope with her name on it. She placed her papers and her bag on the desk, and opened up the envelope. She read the note, as she sat down, and realized it was from Lars. She sat there, after reading it, and began to absorb what he had done. Her thoughts trailed for a few minutes: "*..He probably feels that he is a prophet..., but, ironically, Mom and Dad got closer, and I wonder if they just might like each other again...Anyway, the Lord works in mysterious ways, could it be that he was used to allow us to heal from this breakup? Who knows...But, what do I do, now? ...Do I call him to ask him why? I think I need to get past this...*"

The rest of the day was a blur. She remembered feeling slightly depressed but regained her composure, when the deacon informed her that he had prayed with the lady, she had recommended prayers for.

Proceeding with life after such an experience, can be a learning tool, or a traumatically difficult event to overcome. From the whole family perspective, with a faith-based mindset, it may have been the boost needed to return to normalcy.

As Sino relived the day, she felt grateful to not have had any impulse in deepening her feelings with Lars.

Around the same time, Roi's emotions were almost to the breaking point. He felt confident that his family would return. Praying for a miracle was a priority on his mind. He didn't feel too concerned that Mota had been angry with him, when he proclaimed that a conversation with Lars was needed, and he had planned to dine with him just to get to know what type of person he was; he was also not too worried about the fact that he had asked her if she was dating anyone; and he was definitely not taken by the fact that Tori was still very mad at him for intervening in her business. He knew however, that his family's well being was the only important thing on his mind.

What kept him going was the knowledge that all was happening for a good reason. Besides, his daughters were not damaged by any of this. A medical report, comprising of a physical and emotional assessment concluded such. All three had undergone one week of psychoanalysis, with the result being found totally conclusive. Biamu had displayed traits of withdrawal, mildly, and feelings of betrayal and hurt; but not any emotional pains that would have lasting effects.

He did meet with Lars to ask him questions about his family and the reasons for his major deception. Although he had a particular profile in mind about Lars' personality, it was determined from his point of view that Lars equated himself to the Gods of yesteryears. His analysis of the conversation led him to believe that he would consult Lars' father to reveal his opinion on his son's state of being.

What resonated mostly from his conversation was Lars' response to the question of Why did you do this?

His response was *"..With all due respect, Sir, I think you need to understand that nothing is planned in this world. What happened in your life is what you should be concerned with. I am willing and able to marry any of your daughters, if you so allow..."*

To which, Roi responded...

"Son, I am sitting here with you; but, I do not believe you understand the gravity of what you have done.., Frankly, I really feel that a breaking point has been presented to you, so that you do not repeat the same mistake... As far as marrying one of my daughters, I would have to reject that possibility..."

Lars simply looked away, and gestured that he understood, with his right thumb up.

Roi was very glad to have met a young man, whose notion of life was to justify the means to an end. He, just like Sino, wondered if he was placed in his path for a specific reason.

The days of reminiscing permeated for a while within all concerned. Arias was elated to have played a role in the development of things. Tam became less and less concerned when Mota made her affirmations that all was well with her daughters. Biamu and Tori laughed a lot together as they compared notes about Eon Aron. Sti kept in close contact with Mota and quoted scripture often every time she spoke to her, reiterating how everything that was happening was a sign from above. She was adamant about seeing this situation through the end, with the end being a return to normalcy for an up and coming family.

Chapter 10

Sti truly believed that Mota had made an awful mistake by leaving her home, but actually revealed it over and over by speaking on different scenarios of what-ifs.

She was on the phone with Mota making plans for a trip to simply take her mind off things for a while. Arrangements were made for the girls to stay with their father for about a week. She made plans to visit several European cities–Madrid, Paris, Helsinki, etc. She surmised that they would return refreshed with a new outlook. Besides, Biamu and Tori had just graduated from High School and were felt to be on the right path. A self-rewarding experience was needed to proceed forward with plans for the future.

Analytically, it can be said that family bonds that strengthen in times of crises, were strong to begin with. Those bonds that become stronger than before, are recognized to be overall blessings that were meant to do just that. As the story of Mota and her husband moves on, there appears to be one general observation. Her mental processes demanded time not only to absorb that she no longer cohabited with her husband, but to also acknowledge whether or not her marriage was worth keeping.

From the girls' viewpoints, their experience was definitely something to remember always. Their closeness became more apparent, as they acknowledged how such an experience could have been avoided, had they shared happenings in their lives, as trivial as these may have been. They promised to keep in contact and not spare a moment of recognition of facts.

Mota took her time, prior to her trip, to explain the delicate balance needed in life; and how precious life can be at one moment; and totally destroyed, the next. She explained how much she understood how they were spared from emotional distress, perhaps from her faith, or some other conduit. But, what remained clear was the lack of dialogue. She made them promise to communicate openly to her, and each other, as they venture out to their college days.

The different types of turmoil presented in Mota's life give rise to the notion that at times, only a miracle can save the day. But, what kind of miracles would be satisfactory in such a case. A bonus of $35,000, unmentioned, triggered the need to separate and kept apart, for mental relief; a husband's personality that is not understood, filters through the minds of his entire family, as being unacceptable, and difficult to grasp; remarks that are hard to comprehend permeate, and simply result in a decimation in depth; but, throughout the different scenarios, a man who felt that he had the right to do as he did, and talked his mind whichever way he needed to, kept his stance on approaches that he felt were upright, and good.

No matter how it's interpreted, a miracle had to surface to set a stage on a future that could be everlasting for this family.

Mota was ready for her trip. Her sets of luggage were in the living room, as she looked around to ensure all was in order. She waited for her transportation to the airport–she planned to meet Sti there, rather than drive herself. As she waited, her phone rang. "Hi Mom,.ready to go now"...

"Yes, I am waiting for my driver...are you three settled in?"

It was Tori, calling to ensure all was well.

"Yes, we are. but, What's with Bromar?"

"What do you mean?"

"She is always so proper around Dad. I think she is scared sometimes..."

"Apparently, there was an episode with some type of disrespect...and you know how Roi can be obnoxious..."

"Wow, that's so mean...what did he do...?"

Chapter 10

"Why don't you ask him what he did...listen, I have to go now, my driver is here. I will call you three, when I get there..."

"Ok, have a nice trip...Bye..."

Mota was definitely on her way, feeling slightly happy to get away for a while. Her driver came in, took her luggage, placed them in the trunk; opened the back door on the driver side, waited for Mota to come down.

When she finally came in the car, the driver closed the door; got in, and drove off.

At the airport, it only took a few minutes to find Sti, waiting for her. They hugged and walked to the nearest shop to purchase a few necessities, e.g. extra napkins, silk sleep masks, and aspirin. Although the flight was to last for about seven hours, they planned on being prepared for possible emergencies and unexpected landings elsewhere.

They had more than enough time to relax before their flight, so they found a small pub at the airport. They chatted there about different things involving the kids' stay with Roi; Bromar's situation; incidents regarding Lars and Biamu, (mostly); and again a $35,000 bonus which was not explained to her, as to why it was not disclosed. What angered her more, was the fact that, as far as their finances were concerned, Mota was always in charge, throughout their marriage. Hidden from her, without a clear explanation, felt like embezzling funds, for the purpose of deceiving.

"He did tell me briefly he would explain his rationale for not revealing anything about this money"

"...Well, in that case, wait and see what he says. It could turn out to be absolutely nothing."

"I don't think so. The look on his face, when I confronted him about it, said it all. I think he probably has some secret projects he's working on, not involving me in it..."

"At this point, Mota, do you really mind what he was doing... remember, you left the house, without his approval...actually, let me rephrase that, without his agreeing with you, on that.So, think of it as an event of the past, if you should disagree with his explanation of it."

"I'll see if I can..."

They conversed, back and forth; agreeing and disagreeing. On their conversation regarding Biamu, Sti expressed her deepest feelings on seeing that she was not a victim of passion. Mota explained that after a head to head conversation with Biamu, she surmised that nothing really serious happened. Biamu did confess that she was beginning to fall madly in love; and felt glad to have been rescued.

As soon as it was time to board the plane, they both dragged their wheeled luggage to their respective counters; then boarded.

Their flight was pleasant. Mota slept during most of it. They landed during the early evening hours. After picking up their luggage from the point of discharge, they dragged most of it along to summon a cab to their destination.

A short trip from the airport to their hotel would have taken only 45 minutes. They felt that something was terribly wrong, as the car kept jerking along the road, and suddenly stopped.

Meanwhile, at the house, Tori kept her observance on her father and Bromar. She knew that somehow there was so much fear on Bromar's part that it could not be ignored. So, she mentioned her observations to Biamu, who along with her sensed that there was some kind of discipline taking place.

"Do you feel what I am feeling, about this girl. She seems like a different person when Dad walks in the room..."

"I think she has issues..."Biamu responded

"Let's just ask her what's going on...mom said there was a disrespect episode that went on..."

"Ok. Let's ask her."

Both Tori and Biamu kept at it, and finally asked her point blank. "Why are you afraid of him. He is not going to hurt you..."

At that question, Bromar maturely responded: "What he did for me, may have saved my life"

The questions that filtered through the girls' minds were somewhat perplexing. But, she explained that she realized she was on the wrong path, smoking pot, going to racy places, and making the wrong kinds of friends. " Even though I still miss doing these things, I think I prefer his approach much more than living at my own place."

Tori and Biamu kept quiet and did not even ask specifically what he had done to transform her into a scared little thing. They continued their conversation exchanging ideas on how she could be totally normal with Roi, just like they were. She declined, and jumped to another conversation. While doing so, she did mention: ..."No one needs to go through life, cleaning up after other people until they're into their adulthood..."

Both Tori and Biamu were even more perplexed, and promised that they would tackle the situation with their dad, in full force.

Meanwhile, Overseas, Mota and Sti sat in their cab, waiting for another driver to rescue them from a stalled vehicle with engine troubles. They kept looking at their watches, wondering when they could actually unwind from such a long trip. "Do you know what I am thinking?"

"No, don't even say it..."Mota answered.

She knew exactly what Sti's next statement would be, regarding how things worked, as messages from above. They kept quiet, waiting. Finally, after close to two hours, a huge suburban pulled up, and stopped right in front of their vehicle.

They walked out, and got into the suburban, after verifying with the initial driver, that the new driver was indeed the one they were waiting for.

They reached their destination within 30 minutes; dragged their light luggage sets with them, and allowed the bellboys to help out with their bigger sets of luggage. With a generous tip, the driver sped off.

Once they walked up to the reservation desk, to check in, they were informed that their reservations had been canceled, due to delay in arrival time. Sti looked at Mota, and said nothing. "Can you give us any type of similar accommodations. It's really late. We cannot make another reservation with another hotel. Please?"Mota pleaded.

"We have two rooms on separate floors, that we can give you... Is that acceptable?"

"Are these rooms furnished appropriately with the same ..."

Before she finished her sentence, Mota stopped and just said: "Yes, we'll take these rooms..."

Sti looked a bit tired, but on her mind, several verses of scripture were roaming. *"Roi belongs with her. How is it that, we're trying to get away for the sake of revival, after so much turmoil, and we're being bombarded with so many issues. I think these things are downright, true messages from above. This man is a good man. I will tell her my piece even if it's the last thing I do..."*

They took the elevator to their respective floors, and bid good night. But, before they actually parted, Sti told her to call her on her cell when she could. They made a point to keep in touch while unwinding.

Chapter 10

As soon as Mota reached her room, she observed the accommodations were not as grand as she expected, but she felt satisfied. She looked in her handbag and noticed that her credit card was missing. She phoned the front desk and was informed that the card was at the desk, totally ready to be picked up.

Mota took the elevator, and felt a sudden jump on the elevator chords; then it suddenly stopped. She was stuck between floors.

Because of the time difference in the states, compared to overseas, it was early in the morning where Roi was attempting several times to contact Mota. As urgent as it appeared to be, since She had never not called her family when on an outing, Roi was also dealing with accusations of being "super mean"to Bromar. "She is scared to death of you, Dad; how could you do that? What exactly did you do to her?"

Roi disregarded most of the talks from his daughters, and seemed preoccupied with the fact that he left at least three prior messages, without any replies.

Sti, was sound asleep at that time, not hearing her phone ring. She finally heard the sound, and awoke quickly. By the time she picked up, the line was no longer held by the caller. She quickly looked in her caller ID feature, and noticed that it was Roi's number. She redialed, and looked at her watch – it was a little after 11:30PM. "You called. What's going on?"

"I've been trying to get a hold of Mota for the past couple of hours, she is not picking up."

"Roi, it's late, here. Maybe she's sleeping."

"It's not like her, not to let us know she arrived safely."

"Oh, she didn't call you nor the girls?

"No. none of us."

"That's strange. But, come to think of it, she was somewhat upset, that we lost our reservations because of late arrival. she probably got so tired, and simply fell asleep."

"You lost your reservations at the hotel? but why were you so late getting there?"

"Our car had engine troubles. We had to wait for a long time for some other car to pick us up"

"So, you're saying she probably got so tired...I think I want to confirm this...can you try to get in touch with her?"

"I really don't think that's necessary, but, to make you feel better, just hold on, I 'll use the hotel's phone to ring her room."

Sti placed her cell on her bed, and scooped over to the hotel's phone and rang Mota's room.

The phone rang several times. No answer.

Sti rang again, to ensure that she had not dialed a wrong number. Same result.

Sti took her cell phone, and told Roi she would call him back. "I will walk over to her room and knock to see what's going on with her.

"Please call me back ASAP" Click. Roi hung up. But, he was worried.

Sti walked over to her bathroom; splashed some water on her face, and took her cell, as she darted out of her room. She took the elevator up to the 10th floor. The hotel had about seven elevators on different corners of the facility.

Sti reached the room and knocked slightly. No answer. She knocked a little bit more forceful. No answer. She dialed Mota's cell, and heard the ring from outside of the door. No answer. She then dialed Mota's hotel room phone. Still no answer.

She began to knock fiercefully to have her come to the door. Then finally gave up and darted downstairs to the reception area. "I am trying to locate my friend from room 1009. I went to her door and knocked, there's no answer. Where's the hotel manager? I would like to speak to him or her, right now, please."

The receptionist looked at a note that was left for her to give a Credit card to a Mota...; Then, she said, is this in reference to a credit card?someone named Mota..., was supposed to come down and pick up a credit card..."

"So, are you telling me she never made it down here?"

"The card is still here. Wait a minute. I'll talk to my supervisor and see how he can help"

A few minutes passed. Then a well dressed man was hurrying down the corridor toward Sti.

"How can I help you?"

"My friend and I arrived earlier today. Now, I think she is either passed out in her room, or I am not sure what to think. Can you please open her room, to verify whether or not she needs help. It's not like her not to call her family when she is away from home."

"I am assuming you've done everything possible to reach her, and have been unsuccessful. So, now the only alternative is to actually gain entrance to her room and verify her whereabouts. Please come with me."

Sti heard her cell ring as she walked over with the manager. It was Roi. "Have you found her?"

"We're on our way to her room, right now. Just hold on."

The manager and Sti reached the room. He knocked gently. No answer. He knocked forcefully. No answer. He took out his phone to notify a hotel Exec, that he had to gain entrance to a guest's room. He kept the line open, as he opened the door. Sti rushed in thinking she would see her on her bed, snoring. She wasn't there. Her handbag, as well as her unopened luggage were on the bed. Sti walked over to the bathroom. Nothing was touched. It was as if absolutely no one had occupied the room. The manager was baffled and said there was an inquiry regarding a credit card; perhaps she had gone somewhere else before actually appearing at the front desk. Sti's thoughts were so intense, that she completely disregarded Roi's questions on the line. "Have you found her? Is she all right?"

Sti's thoughts were ravaging her being–The manager's questions were left up in the air."*She called about her credit card...all she took with her was her key to the room...she left her cell here, her handbag, filled with cash..., she simply wanted to fetch her card...*"

Remembering that Roi was on the line, Sti quickly updated Roi "...I am sorry to say...there is a problem...She is nowhere to be found...the manager is here...we are going to figure this out...apparently, she just wanted to go pick up her credit card... but, she never made it down there..."

"Sti, you're not making any sense. Where is Mota? should I come over there?"

"No, No, I just thought of something..., Roi, I'll ring you right back."

Sti stormed out of the room, leaving the manager wondering what could have happened. Then she began to retrace Mota's steps, and empathized that if it had been her, she would have taken her room key, and gone to the elevator, to reach the lobby area.

Then, she thought..."*the elevator.*"

Then she quickly asked the manager. "How many elevators are on this floor?"

For the past couple of hours, Mota was between floors. She realized it was a dire situation, and remained calm. After pressing the emergency button, and not hearing any sounds, she knew she was in trouble. She screamed out "Help" for more than 30 minutes, straight. To no avail. She began to feel so worn out, that she sat on the floor of the elevator, hoping to be rescued. She resumed her screams again. Nothing. She fell asleep slightly and dreamed that she had reached the red bricked cathedral in Helsinki. Her dream was to visit the natural museum, there. But, what she saw was the museum within the cathedral. The scenery of the church was combined with that of the museum. She was walking toward the pulpit; then a priest, robed in white and red, stopped her from reaching further. He had a gavel in his right hand, and banged it several times, near the tabernacle, he kept banging it, and banging it...then all of a sudden, Mota woke up; opened her eyes, and kept hearing the banging. But, this time, she heard Sti's voice, saying..."Mota, are you down there? answer me please" the banging continued. She was so dehydrated, that she could not even respond. With all her might, she began to pound the elevator wall to the right of her. Sti immediately called out one more time..."The manager is calling for help...Hang on..."

Sti was feeling elated, joyful with tears, while calling Roi. "We found her. She was stuck in between floors on an elevator."

"Good grief!...To think that we all were having a grand old time, while my wife was stuck, feeling every ounce of danger... Can you put her on the line, please?"

"No, Roi, the manager is calling someone to fix the problem. She is not out yet. I will call you as soon as she comes out..."

With trembling voice, Roi said: "Do that, please."

Sometimes, in life, the recognition of a miracle, in the midst of turmoil is wise. In this particular case, a woman whose idea of reaching a level of calmness by traveling far away from home, has found a different set of issues, temporary or not, which must be dealt with.

The both sided effect of the miracle, began with the moment Roi heard that Mota was missing. Upon hearing such, he gasped and literally aged right before his daughters' eyes. At which point, Tori blurted out: "...did you say mom was missing?"He, in response, laid the phone down on the table, and opened his arms, gesturing them to come over closer, and began to sob. All three were in shock, and questioned everything, about what would happen next; how they were going to deal with the fact that their mom was missing. Their questions could not be answered by Roi. He simply stated: "Sti will call back if there's any change." The girls felt closer to their father, more so than they had ever felt. Tori saw the tears in her father's eyes, and began to weep. Sino and Biamu held each other; while Bromar, who had no idea what had transpired, said nothing, but joined them all, with sadness on her face.

On Mota's side, a miracle was forming in her head. As she waited for her rescuers, she began to feel that God was punishing her, for not having listened to Sti. She began to utter to herself, *"are we in Finland?"* She felt delusional. With so many moments of fear experienced, Mota was very taciturn and just wanted to sit there and wait. Although she heard Sti's voice, reassuring her that all was well, she was too exhausted to speak.

In the wake of a situation such as that, an analysis may sometimes be required to somehow comprehend the rationale behind what transpires. It could very well be an instance of misguidance, or a self-fulfilling prophecy of some sort; or even just an event from spontaneity. No matter what the analysis may reveal, it stands clear that understanding the dynamics of any situation is essential.

From Mota's state of mind of acceptance, by waiting for a rescuer to arrive; and knowing that a good friend was out there, conveying messages to her family, she remained absolutely confident that all would turn out fine. In her self reflection, she began to feel anxious about her relationship with her husband; and whether or not such a relationship could be redeemed or salvaged.

In a marriage where the existence of the unforgivable, is not there, the possibility of a revival and reconciliation is always present. From not being able to understand the retention from knowledge of a bonus; to raw statements here and there; and a personality that projects a continuity of an unbearable affront, it can be said that the challenge to a peaceful coexistence is ever present. However, with different developments that can ultimately strengthen and fortify their bonds, the likelihood of a unified bliss can surface.

As soon as Mota heard a commotion around the area, she felt relieved and anxious to again resume her normalcy. The only issue was such that her sedentary position on the floor for more than two hours affected her blood circulation to the point of stiffness around her legs. A combination of shock, fear, acceptance of the worst, somehow created a variety of mental conflicts. But, the real truth on her mind related to the fact that she would be rescued; then she would examine her life in depth, and she would commit to studying the word more and more. Her thoughts trailed for a while; then she felt sleepy. However, her sleepiness translated into a partial restoration of her mind; as she began to feel the elevator moving, and a great deal of noise around it. As soon as the elevator door opened, Sti reached out to her, and said "Easy..."to the paramedics, the firemen, and all others associated with the repair of the elevator. "Are we in Finland?" she groggily asked. They took her on a gurney, and checked her pulse and all other vital signs, and wheeled her away. Sti responded: ..."No, not yet. But, I promise you, we'll get there." As she ran alongside the paramedics, she called Mota's family, whose anxiety grew by the minute. As soon as Roi answered, Sti informed him of what was going to happen, "We're on our way to the hospital. But, she seems fine..., slightly groggy, but, fine..."

"May I speak to her, please?"

"She is resting now..., just hold on."

Sti got in the ambulance, and asked if she could just say "hello" to her husband. The medic advised against that. "We gave her a sedative. It would be wise not to disturb her right now. We're treating her for shock."

"Can you speak to her husband, and explain to him? because he really wants to speak to his wife. He is worried."

"Certainly" He took the phone from Sti. "Sir, I understand how you feel. But, please know that we're doing the best that we can to treat her delicately. She absorbed some type of shock. But, I think she is fine. We're taking her to a hospital, and will be released..."

"Is she injured physically in any way?"

"No, she isn't. She is slightly delusional...asking about Finland...but, that's the extent of her mental state. It's common for these types of instances..."

The conversation lasted just for a few minutes. Roi felt reassured that his wife was fine. His children were elated that all was well. "...But, why can't she speak to us?" Tori asked.

Roi explained the situation by reassuring them all, that based on his conversation with the paramedic, it's common procedure that they refrain from allowing patients to speak to others during transport. "We'll talk to her soon."

This whole saga represented a breaking point for the family. It was surely a point derived from an opportunity to unite. Roi and his children were somewhat in sync with their feelings, representing a common bond. As Mota was felt to be missing, somehow, her family sensed that there would be reason to hope for the best to occur. Tori, at one point, could not stop crying, holding on to her father, who similarly could not retain his usual stance on rigidity. His breakdown was surprising to his children, as well as Bromar, whose mind was racing relative to the human side of Roi. His weakness was in full display. He truly loved his wife.

After close to the end of the day, while it was daylight, overseas, Sti was by Mota's bedside. "I am truly fine. I knew that eventually I would be rescued; but I still felt frightened..."

"...You're looking well. I am glad. Thanks be to God, for blessing you with a husband like that."

"What do you mean...?"

"Without his persistence, you would still be on that elevator..."

"...He didn't receive a call from me..., I always call when I am away..."

"...well, my dear friend, your routine paid off..., because I was in my bed, snoring, when he insisted on calling me..."

"...where's my phone? I need to hear their voices, too...and tell them I am really ok."

"You can use mine. Yours is somewhere with your other effects..."

As soon as she reached the hospital, she was disrobed, and provided with hospital attire. That and her phone were placed in a locker nearby.

During Mota's conversation with her husband, it all seemed to get into place. He promised he would explain his rationale for not having disclosed the bonus money which she found to be unforgivable. The last part of the conversation ended with "...when I tell you why I didn't reveal it, you will be pleased."

Mota stayed on her bed wondering what could have possibly been the reason for his silence on such a big bonus. But, with the promise she made to herself on repairing her life, she remained silent during that part of the conversation and conveyed that she was ready to listen without judgment.

The miracle of full reconciliation was at play in certain aspects. While Mota was adamant about her mental boundaries, she became more and more willing to compromise somewhat and fully grasp her husband's personality.

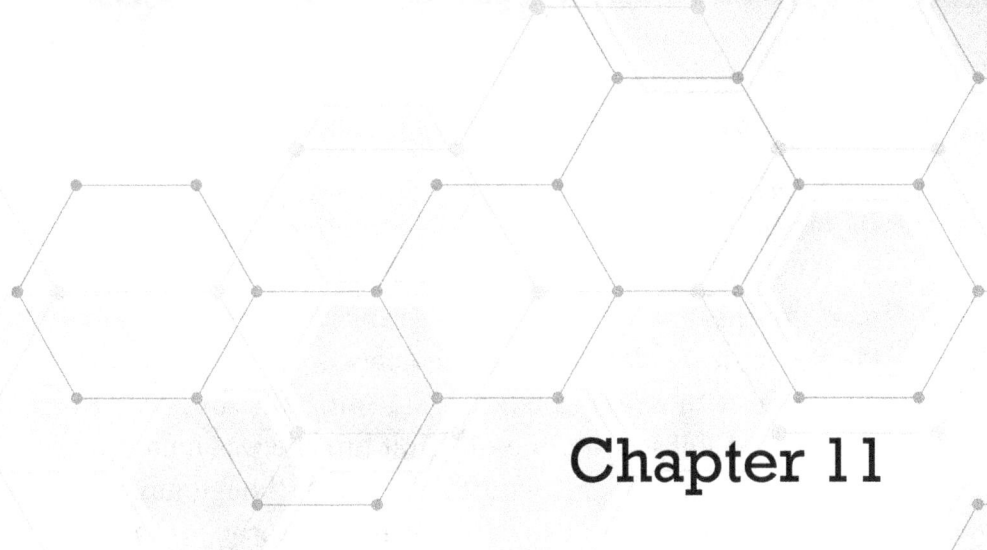

Chapter 11

Triumphantly, at last
Roads, although somewhat twisted
Leading further away from the past
Projecting outlook not wasted

During times of crises, it can be said that every-thing, including feelings, values, routines, what we hold dear sentimentally, becomes a matter of pride, and gratitude. Particularly, when the end result is surprisingly pleasant for all concerned. While this man felt affected by the departure of his family, he maintained his self confidence that eventually he would prevail in winning the trust of the people he loved and cherished in this world.

He felt rejuvenated since Mota had conversed with him every day, during her trip. She had been released by the hospital, a few days prior, and managed to keep her itinerary for the trip. Just like Roi, her children kept in close contact with her, every day. On the day of her arrival back to the states, Roi was somewhat preoccupied by an issue involving a woman named Somti.

On the very day his wife was to return from her overseas trip, he received the phone call from her, he felt a bit concerned, considering what he had been through a few years prior, with this person.

He sat in his living room, reliving the day he heard her name for the first time. An issue regarding his friendship with Martin arose. According to this woman, the birth of Bromar coincided with a time when Roi had some kind of ties with her mother. Roi's memory of the first time he was unfaithful to his wife came back in full force. Within his thought process of the first time he spoke to Somti, he filtered through the first time he met Bromar's mother. He remembered sitting at a bar when someone named Luet, came and sat about two stools from him. He started a conversation with her. One thing led to another; then they met at a resort for two days. He lost contact with her for several years; but, was shocked to meet her again, as Martin's wife. Although he chose not to mention anything to Martin, he never once attempted to cheat on his wife again. Martin and Luet divorced, because of her infidelity, that was felt to be unbearable by Martin.

Around the 10th birthday of Bromar, The Somti person attempted to blackmail Roi, into giving her a large sum of cash to keep quiet about the possibility of having fathered her. He remembered part of the conversation: "*...How would you like me to tell Mota everything, Hmmm...?*

"*You can do as you please. I know for a fact that the girl is not mine...*"

"*she will be mad with you when she finds out that you cheated on her while she's away on a business conference...I swear, all you men are just a bunch of %%#%%#s..., you don't deserve to be married happily while you're getting your groove on...*"

That part of the conversation gave Roi an immediate headache as he was remembering. Out of curiosity, he did have tests done secretly to ensure that Bromar was not his. A few years, prior, a good friend of his, who held medical degrees performed paternity tests, without Martin's knowledge, to somehow alleviate any worries that he was experiencing.

So, as he sat there in his living room, counting the hours, for his wife to return, he felt instantly worried. *"what does she want now? Why is she calling me...?"*referring to Somti.

The message that she left was somewhat fierce. "Hello Roi, I think I need to talk to you. No need to call me back. I will do so when I am good and ready."

The fact that he had been through such a tumultuous period in his life, coupled with the anxiety surrounding recent traumatic sessions, producing a teachable moment, left him in urgent need of calmness and serenity. He paced back and forth, but his thought process was alarming to the point of his blocking any conversation conducted with him. Tori had to call out Dad, Dad,...a few times, before he acknowledged her. "...Oh, I am sorry..., What do you need?"

"We need to go to the airport..., now, otherwise, we will be late..."

"...You're absolutely right...I'll be ready in a sec."

He walked upstairs, and got to his bedroom, still feeling a certain element of guilt for his past mistakes. He remembered Mota's reaction when she knew how unfaithful he had been. It took about three weeks for him to be allowed back into the house. With his constant requests for forgiveness for having had weakness of the flesh, Mota finally forgave him, but kept close eyes to their financial affairs. When the bonus was not revealed, not only did she feel there may have been another episode of his deceit, she also felt betrayed. True to her feelings, in reality she knew he would never be unfaithful again, but, remained totally alert to such a possibility.

Roi's mind was blurred into different directions as he pondered what could be on Somti's mind. He became totally alert when Tori, one more time, screamed out…, "..Dad, we're going to be late…"

Meanwhile, Mota and Sti were elated to have had a "Not so bad"European trip. They chatted quite a bit about the outcome of what could be termed as a disaster to remember on their first day. They, however, felt grateful that somehow all worked out. The pilot of the plane directed all to take their seat, as the plane descended to land.

Roi and his daughters, on the way to the airport, felt certain that a new beginning was on the horizon. Tori, especially, noticed how cozy things seemed when her parents chatted every day, talking about old times. She overheard part of a conversation that ended in "…I can't wait to see how things turn out…We can find happiness again…etc…" She fully understood her mom's rationale for having left; but was never made aware of the specifics, including his past infidelity. She knew for certain that she loved her father. Had it not been for the fact that her mother was missing at one point, she would not have felt the type of sentiments that emerged during the climax of the problem. A certain type of fear resonated with her, in terms of what would transpire when they live as a family again.

Both Sino, and Biamu, were busy reading, and seemed totally upbeat about the possibility of seeing good family times again.

As Roi drove, different sceneries were played on his mind. He felt himself practicing how he would explain the bonus, without delving into extreme details. After all, he still worked for his company. "…*A good company…, with a few bad apples.., my retirement and pension plans will be there for me to enjoy…*

after all these years..., but, there are certain things that I will not stand for...besides, at my age..."

The thoughts kept him alert, analyzing, while driving at the same time.

When they reached the airport, it was just at relatively the same time, Mota and Sti landed.

The joy of having had a good landing after a long flight is probably one of the most pleasant experiences of all time. Such sentiments appeared to permeate around the aircraft, as passengers stood up to stretch their legs, sighing to savor their surroundings of calmness and goal reaching.

Sti and Mota walked toward the luggage area, to fetch their belongings. On the way there, Sti quoted several verses of scripture to reassure Mota that her decision to consider saving her marriage was the right one. She quoted 2nd Corinthians 5:17 – "...Anyone who belongs to Christ has become a new person. The old life is gone. A new life has begun..." She also quoted 1 John 4:18"...such love has no fear; because perfect love expels all fear..."and felt proud reciting these verses. Mota listened and nodded several times. They took their luggage and walked toward the lobby area to reach Mota's family. Sti bid goodbye; since her car was left on the Airport lot, and waved at the family, as she reminded Mota of a meeting that was to be held soon. The girls waved as well; as Roi walked over to his wife and hugged her.

A short distance between the airport and Mota's rental was measured at less than seven miles. They reached, as Sino walked out to stay with her mom. But, the two girls, Biamu and Tori decided they would stay with their father, for the day. While traveling in the car with them, Mota's excursions sounded adventurous, as she detailed the various sites she visited. She recalled being in the walking district in Barri Cotic, in

Barcelona; Taking the TAP carrying passengers on Porto route in Lisbon; Being at the national park in Finland, etc. Roi was elated to hear that the trip had been a success. He promised to take her and the whole family to the Caribbean, sometime, in the future.

When they reached, Mota expressed that there were some loose ends she needed to tie, with respect to her feelings. She also reminded Roi about the bonus explanation which she could not wait to hear about. Before leaving, Roi simply said: "When are you coming home?"

To that, she responded,…"…I am not rushing back; but, be assured that things have gotten clearer on my mind…just give me time…"

"Can we meet tomorrow to have a talk about things…?"

"Yes. Let's do that in the afternoon. Have an appointment with a psychologist…in the morning"

For the rest of the day, Sino stayed with her mother; while the other two stayed with their father. Although there had been no discussions regarding a possible full reconciliation of both parents, all three sensed there would be some sort of friendship that could lead to cohabitation.

While in the company of her mother, sitting in the family room, Sino asked several questions related to marriage, and why two people simply could not stay together. Case in Point: Her bible study friend, who seemed genuinely unable to reconcile the differences that surfaced during her marriage. Mota explained that such a commitment is very serious. But, at times, the devotion on one side, exceeds the other side so tremendously, that it becomes virtually impossible to bring the expectations of both side to an equilibrium, creating an imbalance of some sort. Sino was still confused; but understood the concept that her mother was attempting to express. "…Why, then, do you and my father separate? you seem to be at a crossroad for furtherance of the relationship...19 years, is a long time..."

"I realize that. Something always keeps me from totally separating from him...Do you realize that since I've left the house, we've communicated at least twice a week?"

"...Wow, I didn't know that. It proves that you belong together...I know Dad can be quite a character; but I love him more than hate what he does..."

"...I know. It can be difficult. I need to be sure of what I am feeling before going back."

"Will you go back to him? And When?"

"I really can't say yet."

Mota's conversation with her daughter was deep, in terms of the reassurance sought from Sino. In a separation, it is indeed true that the offsprings are the ones who are affected the most.

On the other side of town, Tori and Biamu were asking the same thing of their father. He ended the conversation with."... Mota and I have a strong bond. I don't believe that she will leave, because I am, after all, a good husband..."With a smirk on his face. Both Biamu and Tori just looked at each other, wondering if their Dad would ever understand the initial reason why their mother left him, in the first place. Tori's thoughts trailed..."...*He still sounds sarcastic...and pompous...God, help us...*"

The rest of the day was normal, with Bromar feeling relieved that Mota enjoyed her mini vacation, despite her dilemma; and Biamu wondering if ever her parents actually reconciled for good, if she would experience the same trauma, all over again.

In life, at times, it can be rewarding to revert to a previous state, when an adverse experience allows such to occur. With the myriad of issues presented, a weak mind would have been long gone, without the possibility of resuming life as it once was. In this particular case, Both Mota, and Roi, from a strong personality, somehow sensed a deeper connection within themselves, to hold on to their bond, not only for their children, but also for their own interests, emotional, or otherwise.

The following day, after having attended her therapeutic session, Mota felt relieved and decisive. She replayed in her mind, the words of the therapist–"...*We have to find empathy, and compassion when dealing with a mate; we must also lay out the pros and cons for the rationale that we place in holding on. In all likelihood, if the pros exceed the cons, it is worthwhile to keep holding on. In your case, I fully understand how you feel. But, 19 years, is a long period, in which you could have decided to end it all; but, you didn't. The decision to work it out is not in my hands...*" She also kept remembering the little voice in her head, saying, that she should make the right decision. After her meeting with the psychologist, she knew that given the right explanation for the bonus, she would indeed resume living with her husband, under acceptable conditions.

Although the idea of listing the pros and the cons appealed to her, she did not actually list anything; but, on her mind, she knew the pros were in excess of the cons. Particularly, the kind of father he represented for her girls. His compassion, patience, and skills in disciplining were very important, as she replayed the many times, he counseled the girls about things. At times, it would be unnerving, but somewhat understood to be silly, at best.

On the same front, all three of their daughters, began to analyze a different perspective on their parents' marriage. Tori's thoughts were leaning toward a possibility that they loved each other so much, that psychologically, their mother's irritation was to bring her marriage to perfection. Biamu's thoughts emphasized that a two parent household resulted in a greater chance for stability, respect, and sense of direction. To her, she wished that her father had been with them, when Aron walked into her life. She felt that things would probably have been different. Sino's notion of life was to engage in biblical studies. Although she felt much more closer to her mom, her father's presence always illuminated her life in ways she simply could not explain.

Mota was totally prepared for her meeting with Roi. She made mental notes on what explanations she would accept versus which ones she would not. As she began to think about the detriment of grasping the wrong message from the upcoming session with Roi, on his revelations, she felt slightly frightened.

Roi, on his end was getting ready to drive over for his meeting with Mota, when his phone rang. "Hello"

"Hi, it's me. Can I talk to you?"

"Somti, what do you want?"

"I know you don't think much of me, or what I want to say, but, one thing for sure, I know you must be loaded with all those bonuses you got..."

"Excuse me..."

"...First of all, I know you received close to $80K, for that thing that was going on..."

"Look, if you think you can get away with blackmailing me for what's going on in that little head of yours, you are mistaken...do you hear me? Stop calling me to talk about nonsense

Now, I need to know what you want..."

"...I just need financial help with a project. I need you to be my partner..."

"...The answer is NO. One other thing: I didn't receive $80K from anyone. Get your facts straight..."

"If you don't talk to me now. I know you will talk to me later on..."

"What are you talking about?"

"...I will call you again..."

"Please don't"

Click.

Roi was so irritated, that he became slightly worried.

He, nonetheless drove to Mota's rental, for his meeting with her. He reached on time, and was greeted at the door, by Mota, smiling and telling him to come in.

She offered him tea, biscuits, and light snacks. He was still very shaken by Somti's strategy. One thing that left him wondering was – timing. *"Why did she call me today about bonuses, when I have to meet with Mota, to talk about this $35K issue? Strange..., but linked...anyhow, this person needs to get out of my life."*

Mota knew her husband well, and noticed that he had plenty on his mind. After a few small talk sessions, she blurted out– "Now, can we talk about the bonus money you hid from me"?

"Yes. How can I put it?this money I haven't spent it...it is still a check..."

"Why didn't you deposit it? That's what I am confused about..."

"I understand. You see, I don't intend to keep it..."

"Why not?"

"There were a few issues going on at the company. I suspect that these issues had some illegalities..."

"What kind of illegality?"

"..I signed off on the termination of two Execs, Tahaliz and DarpLynn, two HR Execs. Usually, when I sign off on these things, I have to have the correct papers to do so. At this instance, a guy who was the lead investigator didn't furnish me with any paperwork on the rationale for firing these two people..."

"So!..are you saying you received a bonus for their termination?"

"Precisely... But, I needed some sort of evidence to take to Ollie, to somehow explain the reason for not accepting the bonus..."

"Why do you want to work at that company, if things like that are going on...?

"...It's a good company. The CEO is an ethical fellow, who does not allow any kind of shady things at the company. Just a few bad apples..."

"...When will you return the check? if that's what you still want to do?"

"...Of course I will return it...in due time..."

"Why didn't you tell me about this?"

"I didn't know how to tell you. I still have a problem with something else. There's a woman named Somti, who is trying to blackmail me..."

"Blackmail?"

"Yes. She called me right before I came here..."

"Why? What does she want?"

"...A partnership, in some project that she is building up..."

"I don't follow. What does she have on you?"

"It's a long story. But, let me ask you this. Did you tell anyone about my meeting you here today? To discuss the bonus problem?"

"No, Except Sti; because she is always so concerned about what's going on with me..."

"...Ok. This Somti person...Have you heard of her from anyone...?"

".Somti...Somti...-...No. Going back to the blackmail problem... what exactly does she have on you?"

"She has nothing on me. She seems to know what goes on in the company. She mentioned a bonus of $80K..."

"What bonus of $80K is she referring to?"

"That's what I want to know..."

Going back and forth wondering what blackmailing really meant in Roi's life, Mota kept thinking *there's no way she could have something so drastically severe that empowers her to blackmail...that's illegal...who is she? Why is she doing this?* The thoughts came and went, with each one, placing Mota in a state of ponder.

The end of the conversation couldn't come soon enough. Mota decided she knew what to do, to convince herself. Going back to her married life was the best option.

"She will be calling me, she says..."

"I think I'd like to hear what she has to say...Wait a minute,... why don't you leave your cell with me, and I'll speak to her..."

"That's an idea. But, isn't it silly to hold on to my phone, just to hear the demands of a blackmailer?"

"If that will resolve the case, I say, let's do it...besides, why does someone blackmail? It's usually to keep a spouse in the dark,...right?"

"...OK. You've got a point...in that case, let's switch phones. I'll keep yours, and you'll keep mine..."

"I have a lot of important reminders on my phone. So, let's do this...if she does not call within 48 hours, we'll take the cells back and decide that her communication is not that important..."

"...However, you want to handle this..."

Chapter 11

"Something else, Roi, I've made a list of things that I think you should try to change in your personality, in order for this to work..."

"Whatever you say, Mota. My marriage is just as important to me..."

The rest of their dialogue involved how they wanted to help the girls decide on college, what type of therapy should be ongoing...; and how she intended to remodel when she returned home. During the conversation, however, nothing from Mota's viewpoints, was definite. She injected, if we do cohabit again – if we decide it's the best option – if there's no other alternative, etc.–leaving Roi in a state of uncertainty.

They switched phones.

Later that evening, while Roi was reviewing some of his work, he was also concentrating on a couple of projects that were becoming overdue. As a workaholic, he always maintained a certain discipline when it came to his routine. A memo to certain colleagues was due; and other types of training procedures were also in the works. As he continued his quest on catching up, Mota's phone, which was on his desk rang. He looked at the caller ID, it was his number, so he surmised that Mota was calling him. "Hi Mota, anything good?"

"I'd say,...excellently good..."

"I am listening."

"...Apparently, you're being groomed for a top spot in the company..."

"I am lost. Whaaat?"

"Somti called, and expressed that, exactly what she expected was happening..."

"...She meant, she knew you would get involved?"

"Yes. She is a "hidden figure" on the company's behalf."

"What? I never suspected that."

"She revealed that ever since you began working there, your work ethics, and your approaches were precisely what the company was searching for..."

"What about the $80K accusation? She was probably pulling your leg..."

"She wanted to put to rest, rumors that were circulating. Apparently, the company is apprehending all involved in a scam that had been permeating for some time..."

"I suspected something was happening. But, I could never have guessed that would be it..."

"She asked about your infidelity, several years ago. I asked her if she knew about it."

"And...what did she say?"

"She felt impressed that I knew about it and took action against you..."

"Well then..., all's well that ends well...But, I don't understand how she knew when I was going to talk about the bonus with you. She called on that very day..."

"I don't know about that. But, the only person who knew about our conversation was Sti...Come to think of it..., Sti's husband goes to a lodge nearby..., he may have mentioned something about us..., which led to someone in Somti's circle. She sounded really connected.

"Anyhow, I'll believe there's a promotion when it happens..."

"By the way, Roi,...have you read anything I've written so far,...about what changes need to be made?"

"No, I haven't yet. I am bombarded with work..."

"So, it's not a priority?"

"Mota, I am dropping everything, and will do it right now..."

With a smile, Mota expressed she would call again to have him drop off her phone to her.

In a myriad of ways, bonds that cannot be broken are somewhat bound for better or worse. As two people present themselves in the presence of God in holy matrimony, their intent on living their lives can be said to be contractual. In this marriage, absent any sort of major irreconcilable differences, a divorce would have been somewhat senseless.

Sino, who stayed with her mom, after her trip, began to notice a glow about her mom. She wondered if indeed her parents had again found each other. She observed her mom's ways, and was able to see the difference in her demeanor; as if she had never really known her husband until then. She was also pensive, thinking about her last conversation with her bible study friend. ..."*I think things will be different for me, now that there's finally an investigation into what's been happening... Good old post office.., apparently, someone was even trying to get into my Express mail...that is a federal crime, to tamper with U.S. mail...I guess they didn't know that. Anyhow, it could also be the Deacon's connections which triggered it all. The preliminary results seem to uncover that it is not the ex husband...it is someone else...*"Sino replayed the conversation on her mind, and felt glad to have been a part of positive results for this woman's struggles. A predicament that lasted for more than 25 years...A type of situation that can be called abusive, preying, and targeting for profit. She seemed also glad to have heard that her friend would not contemplate getting back into her marriage. After all, her children felt it was better to look forward to the future. As she approached her mom to update her on what she's been working on, she excused herself, by saying, "I am sorry to ask, mom, but are you and dad really getting back together?"

"It looks that way..., provided that he fully understands what I've asked him to do for me..."

"What's that?"

"I gave him a list of things that he needs to change, before I fully agree to get back with him."

"However you do it, mom, I think you should know what happened the day he thought you were missing."

"Oh..., what happened?"

"He, literally aged right in front of our eyes. I thought he was going to collapse, right there...I never saw him get affected like that before. That image will remain with me for a long time."

"Tori told me. I am not surprised. I felt the same way when I thought I would never see him or any of you, again. Sitting in that elevator was, by far, the most frightening experience I have ever had..."

"We were frightened too. When we realized you had been rescued, we all sighed with relief...Are you ever going back on a European trip?"ever?"

"Of course. Just because I had one bad experience.., actually three bad experiences..., it doesn't mean I would not go back. Europe is a beautiful continent..., I hope one day, we can all visit some of the most beautiful cities, there."

"Dad is thinking about the Caribbean..., but, I am glad to see you fully recovered from all the bad experiences..."

"Yes, so am I. So, how are you really doing? I mean after the traumatic drama of Lars?"

"I got over it, fairly quickly. I didn't get too involved. I was so busy with the work of the church; and he did send an explanation, by mail."

"Oh, did he?" Steer away from him... he is definitely a heartbreaker..."

"I know. I can't wait to graduate and get on with my career in the ministry..."

"That's what I want to hear..."

Chapter 11

Mom and daughter chatted throughout the evening, about life in general. Mota explained to her daughter the necessities of loving someone in life; and the boundaries that need to be understood to prevent disastrous ties to others. Sino's level of maturity impressed Mota to the point of wishing that the other two were just like Sino.

On the other side of town, Roi sat pensively on his recliner, after reading the conditions set by Mota. ...*"...She wants me to become a totally different person...how can I not criticize Tam's work..., not listening on my girls' phone calls..., and keeping my tongue tied whenever I feel the need to say something...She wants to kill me...how do I respond to this...I know..., I'll promise to do everything that she wants, and then, since she is expecting me not to react to anything..., I'll keep my paychecks to myself, and pay some of the bills, myself...how about that for a resolution? No, that's asking for trouble...I think I should simply correct myself every time I say something wrong..."* His thoughts on how to deal with what was being asked of him kept dwindling. He acknowledged the problem from the standpoint of a personality conflict, but, somehow felt a certain degree of pressure to change his entire psyche – and that was impossible.

From Mota's side of issues, she simply wanted a revival, and a sort of renewed possibility on just about all aspects of her life. Her mate of several years needed to fully comprehend what she needed. Not only peace of mind, but, joy without any twisted notion; and certainties of right, and normalcy of all things, done and said by Roi.

While Sino was at her desk, reviewing some notes, every now and then, she overheard her mom's phone conversation, and realized that somehow there were positive vibes permeating. At one point, she couldn't help giggling, when she heard...".Well, then, I'll stay here with Sino...you can keep Tori and Biamu...".... The manner in which her mom was expressing herself led her to believe that a light was blinking at the end of the tunnel... then, hearing..."...That's more like it...just to remind you of my decision to return, I would most probably revise some of the terms, if you would at least grasp what I am trying to say..."

Sino stopped listening, and continued with her work on the Harbingers II book. She could not believe some of the revelations about the WTC disaster, and the Goddess Kali, that is considered to be some sort of idolatry. She promised herself that she would continue her work on such an important project to share with her fellow Bible Study class members.

As the day progressed, her mom walked up to where she was, and revealed her desire to start packing. She initially hesitated, but, decided it was time to go home. Sino stopped everything, and hugged her mom for emotional support.

Mota got ready to move out. After a few days of preparing, she ensured that all she needed to accomplish, was accomplished. Her conversations with Sti conveyed positivity, and possibilities she never actually explored. Her constant preaching taught her quite a few things on scripture and the full impact of the word.

Her rental was nearly cleaned out. Her boxes of her items packed were so numerous that at times, she lost count. After organizing her itinerary for her day, she ensured that packers would arrive after placing her effects in boxes, which she did. Sino stayed behind with her throughout this period, and periodically mentioned it was the best decision for the entire family. She also mentioned the fact that she would research a club called "Shake Cred Farcos"which dealt with new beginnings. At times, her mom would stop everything to ask her how she was doing. With gladness on her heart, she would simply say: "Great"

The movers showed up; packed everything in the truck, after counting the boxes, and were ready to go. As Mota and Sino walked out of the house, after ensuring that all was cleaned, they glimpsed at the interior one last time, smiled and walked out. Mota left the keys where she was instructed to leave them. She got in her car, as Sino got in hers, then drove off.

On her way there, her mind was totally clear. She would agree to any apology rendered by Roi, if he were to overstep any bounds set by her, to resume a healthy co-habitation. But, what she observed when she reached her place was totally unexpected.

She parked on the street, to leave the driveway open for the truckers. Sino did the same. They walked together, smiling and happy to have finally come back. She reached the front door which was unlocked, as she requested such from Roi. She noticed how cleaned everything was. Biamu, Tori and Bromar greeted her with loudness, and gladness, as they proceeded down the steps. She was glad to see them all. When she looked up, expecting to see Roi, in casual wear greeting her, she saw Roi, with a piece of luggage, with his cell phone pressed to his right ear. He descended down the steps and directed his steps toward the front door. While holding on to his seemingly over-sized piece with his left hand, he said "hold on"to his listener and said..."Mota, you were right. It was a promotion scheme, all along, but, I really don't want to relocate.., but, anyhow, good to have you home..."then continued his conversation, as he walked toward his car. Mota walked slightly behind him, to ask about the luggage. He got in the car, while conversing, then drove off.

Mota stood there, wondering, *"what just happened here?"*...
he left? he had a piece of luggage...he will never change, will
*he? that was not part of what we talked about..."*Her thoughts
were interrupted by Tori, who said, "Mom, I am glad you're
here...Can you please talk to Bromar? She is still very proper
around Dad."

Mota didn't answer, but knew she had far more important
things to talk about. Her husband may have left because of a
nervous breakdown.

The truckers delivered all of their effects, opened all boxes
and placed everything in its place. They got paid for their hard
work, and left. All four girls kept busy as well as Mota, whose
mind was somewhat roaming around a few notions, but, her
main position remained the same. A couple of hours passed;
then she heard Roi's key in the door. He walked in with the luggage in his right hand, and simply said, "Let me put this away,
I'll be right back" He walked up the stairs, got to the closet,
placed the luggage there, and descended down.

Mota's sense of wisdom ordered her to say nothing. She
wondered if perhaps he had to carry something in the luggage, or perhaps he simply changed his mind, after deciding
to leave her. But, she surmised it could not be so. He came
down, being a somewhat new person. He treated Mota in a
manner that was considered the norm, with an extra approach
to keep the peace. He emptied out his pocket to search for
details of the new promotion. Certain papers which he laid
out on the counter included a receipt for a dry cleaning bill
of close to $900. Then, he found what he needed to find, and
began explaining how Ollie had called him to brief him on his
new duties. But, before he could finish explaining, Mota picked
up the receipt, and said pleasantly, "What's this?"he responded,
Dry cleaning bill for all of my single breasted suits"

Chapter 11

Without asking any more questions, Mota began to realize that the luggage contained his suits which he dropped off at the cleaners. When he returned with the luggage, it was empty, because he had dropped off what it contained.

Looking at at his wife's face, Roi picked up on the confusion, but, said nothing. He continued to talk about his promotion, but there was no absorption, on Mota's mind.

They chatted for a while, as a family. At one time, Mota snoopily looked into the luggage to ensure it was empty, as she had expected. It was.

She walked down the stairwell, with a clear mind and a new set of beliefs that priorities in life involved family bonds, and trust that can be measured in so many different ways. She remembered Sti's revelations and all of the biblical scriptures she quoted about life, and turbulences in relationships. As she remained in remembrance, she realized that indeed, her quest in the past year was purely based on a desire to Escape from Within.

Epilogue

Bromar became more and more normal as she adjusted to the presence of Mota, who allowed her to stay with the family, for as long as she wished.

Roi detailed to Mota his approach in disciplining Bromar, because of her disrespectful ways. Mota understood his approach but warned him of his potentially dangerous exaggeration. However, she expressed her support from the standpoint of diminishing negativity.

Although Bromar had looked like a thirtyish something person on the driveway, she was only a 17 yr old with oldish looks on the day Sti observed her presence for the first time.

Tam visited more often than before, as she detected a slight difference in Roi's personality.

Sti felt glad that finally her wishes came true. Seeing her friend's life resume with normalcy, was comforting, and brought a great deal of joy to her. She did confess that she may have blurted part of Mota's business to her husband. But, every time she visited, her bundle of scripture remained with her, to somehow preach to Mota, while ensuring that Mota kept her understanding of the Word of God. The word, through his Son and the Holy Spirit.

Sino received a golden Bible from Lars, with a note that it was a pleasure to see "how dedicated she was in conveying the word of God."

Usam and Lars became closer than ever before; as Usam made it a point to monitor his brother's every move.

Arias' plans for his future laid out specifics on attending Art school to become a famous painter. Tam's guidance over his life included her wishes to allow her son to apply his skills and make his own decisions.

During my process of writing this novel, I experienced quite a few spiritual awakenings which led me to believe that somehow, my efforts in conveying biblical messages were being validated. The manifestations of Almighty God in each life take different forms, in accordance with what each person does on a routine basis. The pandemic, with all of its wonders, worsened my habits of watching television, and as a result, messages of worth may have been transmitted to me through movies that were not necessarily chosen beforehand, or placed on my watchlist. For example, on the very day I updated my manuscript to include an elevator issue, as well as a dream revealing a cathedral, I randomly picked a movie called "5 flights up" Such a movie included an elevator issue, and the mentioning of a cathedral. At another time, an update on infidelity was directly linked to a same day random pick of a movie called "The bay of silence", revealing an infidelity issue, and forgiveness. At another time, an update regarding a promotion for the main character, was somehow observed to be linked to a random pick of a movie called "The terminal", where part of the movie dealt with the mentioning of a promotion. Also around the same period, I painted a piece of Art, containing five trees. On the same day, I randomly picked a movie called "Lady J" depicting on the very first sceneries, five trees.

My decision to write spiritually based books, is not only a therapeutic approach in dealing and coping, such an endeavor allows me to contribute and somehow take part in the human experience. What serves as a relief for the betterment of self, I cannot disregard; but cherish and appreciate as a blessing.

Also in the process of writing this book, I encountered severe hacking attempts, forcing me to utilize various computers to prevent loss of work. These attempts were meant perhaps to discourage me from continuing my quest of writing. In this publication, I explored quite a few issues to convey a different perspective. These issues include the plight of poor communication that can trigger resentment within a family structure; unintentional divisiveness causing a choice of one parent over another; strength in making a decision; courage of a woman to foster; training in the area of law enforcement; an ideal friendship; essential assistance in helping a distressed person over a past marriage, etc, and most importantly the ties of biblical scripture to various developments in life.

My hope is to convey a message of positivity to uplift during current times. As much as I would tend to embark on a string of twists and turns, I find that a readership, with all types of demands can appreciate a sense of uncertainty as well as simplicity. If this book serves as a conduit to elevate understanding in certain issues, I believe that my goal for my writing has been met. Thanks be to God!

Lady J

CPSIA information can be obtained
at www.ICGtesting.com
Printed in the USA
LVHW020819080721
692105LV00004B/285